"Don't you dare do that, Cassidy!"
Sagan roared.

She froze. "Do what?"

"Look at me as though you're scared to death I'm going to throw you on the floor and ravish your body. Don't you dare be frightened of me." He flung open the door. "Not ever."

Cassidy stomped past him into the house and turned on the lights. "Why don't you yell a little, Sagan? Go ahead, shout all you want."

"I'm not yelling," he yelled.

"Oh, do whatever you do want. I don't care diddly-squat what you do."

He began laughing. "Diddly-squat? No one says that."

"It's on par with 'ravish your body,'" she said, poking him in the chest. "Just too corny for words."

"Okay, no more words," Sagan said quietly, and reached for her. Cassidy took a small step back, then stopped. He wrapped her in his arms and with his lips silenced her protests—and the sweet ache inside her. . . .

WHAT ARE *LOVESWEPT* ROMANCES?

They are stories of true romance and touching emotion. We believe those two very important ingredients are constants in our highly sensual and very believable stories in the *LOVESWEPT* line. Our goal is to give you, the reader, stories of consistently high quality that may sometimes make you laugh, sometimes make you cry, but are always fresh and creative and contain many delightful surprises within their pages.

Most romance fans read an enormous number of books. Those they truly love, they keep. Others may be traded with friends and soon forgotten. We hope that each *LOVESWEPT* romance will be a treasure—a "keeper." We will always try to publish

LOVE STORIES YOU'LL NEVER FORGET
BY AUTHORS YOU'LL ALWAYS REMEMBER

The Editors

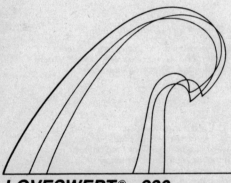

LOVESWEPT® • 230

Joan Elliott Pickart
Illusions

 BANTAM BOOKS
TORONTO • NEW YORK • LONDON • SYDNEY • AUCKLAND

ILLUSIONS

A Bantam Book / January 1988

LOVESWEPT® and the wave device are registered trademarks of Bantam Books, Inc. Registered in U.S. Patent and Trademark Office and elsewhere.

If you would be interested in receiving protective vinyl covers for your Loveswept books, please write to this address for information:

Loveswept
Bantam Books
P.O. Box 985
Hicksville, NY 11802

ISBN 0-553-21859-X

Published simultaneously in the United States and Canada

Bantam Books are published by Bantam Books, Inc. Its trademark, consisting of the words "Bantam Books" and the portrayal of a rooster, is Registered in U.S. Patent and Trademark Office and in other countries. Marca Registrada. Bantam Books, Inc., 666 Fifth Avenue, New York, New York 10103.

PRINTED IN THE UNITED STATES OF AMERICA

O   0 9 8 7 6 5 4 3 2 1

For Anne Madariaga

One

There was a man in her bathtub.

There was a man in her *bathtub?*

Cassidy Cole stared at a spot on the far wall of her living room for a long moment, blinked, then slowly redirected her gaze to the note she held in her hand.

The note itself didn't surprise her. And she rather liked the jungle effect created by the twenty-two plants she'd agreed to care for while her neighbor, Mrs. Henderson, paid a long-awaited visit to her daughter. Mrs. Henderson's instructions came as no surprise, either. Treat the plants with tender loving care, and talk to them every day. It was the final lines of the note that had thrown Cassidy for a loop.

"I put some of the plants by your bedroom window, as you have such marvelous sunlight there. But don't worry, dear. I didn't disturb the man in your bathtub. Tally-ho." Mrs. Henderson always said "tally-ho."

With exaggerated slow motion, Cassidy placed the

note on the end table, along with the extra key Mrs. Henderson had slipped under the door with the note. Then she straightened to her full height, five foot four, and drew a deep, steadying breath. It didn't help one darn bit.

There was not, Cassidy decided firmly, a man in her bathtub. That was insane, absolutely absurd. All she'd done was go out to run a few errands. Things like that didn't happen to ordinary people.

"I must not be an ordinary person," she muttered. Because this was exactly the type of thing that did happen to her. All the time.

"Maybe there's a reasonable explanation for this," Cassidy said to a plant. No, there wasn't. She knew that. There was never a reasonable explanation for the things that happened to her. They just happened. Well, by gum, whoever the twit in her bathtub was, he would have to haul his backside out of there right now.

Cassidy started toward her bedroom, then stopped. Maybe she'd have a cup of tea before she confronted her bathtub buddy. Tea was calming. It would soothe her jangled nerves. Yes, a cup of tea. No, not a cup of tea. She wanted that . . . that whatever he was, out of her bathtub.

Lord, Cassidy thought, what if he was weird; a burglar with a penchant for cleanliness, or a pervert who got his kicks out of sitting in women's bathtubs? Mrs. Henderson had failed to mention if the nut case was *sans* clothes, or if there was water in the tub.

"Well," Cassidy said, tugging decisively on the hem of her sweater, "I'll just check this out." But she didn't move. "Right now."

She could handle this, she told herself. She didn't have a gun, had no training in the martial arts, didn't weigh a breath over one hundred and five pounds, but she had great lungs. Her screams would make a hysterical banshee proud.

Lifting her chin, which was trembling only a tad, Cassidy marched around Mrs. Henderson's plants, into her bedroom, and straight across to the open bathroom door.

And then she stopped. She stopped breathing.

There was, indeed, a man in her bathtub. A naked man.

A man whose head was leaning back against the tiled wall and who was snoring softly. A crummy, rotten bum, who had helped himself to her hot water and her precious Nightly Sins bath crystals, the ones that made huge mounds of fluffy, fragrant bubbles.

A man with a face so tanned, so ruggedly handsome, it was enough to make a woman weep from the sheer beauty of it. Even badly in need of a shave, he was incredible, Cassidy noted. Thick, thick black hair, a straight nose, chiseled cheeks . . . Chiseled cheeks? Yes, chiseled. His face wasn't smooth and refined, but craggy and, oh, Lordy, so darn masculine, it was unbelievable.

Cassidy inched farther into the room, stopping at the edge of the tub. Nice lips, she mused. Kissin' lips, as Aunt Patty would say. Lips made for kissin'. Aunt Patty had said that about Cassidy's lips once, and Cassidy had laughed herself silly. But this man definitely had kissin' lips. Wide shoulders, too—muscled, strong, and so were the arms that disappeared into the bubbles.

The chest, Cassidy decided, was superb, with swirls of dark, moist hair on taut, tanned skin above muscles that just didn't quit.

Her gaze swept quickly downward. Knees. They were bent, indicating he was too tall for the tub. She'd have to take points off for the knees, she supposed. They were a bit knobby. The dab of legs she could see were covered in a smattering of black hair. They looked great, but the knees were nothing to write home about. Well, all things considered, she could forgive him his less-than-wonderful knees.

Enough, Cassidy told herself. Granted, the man was one gorgeous specimen. However! That didn't change the fact that she'd never seen him before in her life, that he was trespassing in all his naked splendor in her bathtub, and that he'd used her Nightly Sins. The very idea. The nerve, the gall, of this man. The next stop his bare bottom made was going to be jail!

"Hey," she said. "Wake up. You, in my bathtub, wake up."

Nothing.

"Yoo-hoo," she called. "Hello? Rise and shine. Up and at 'em."

Nothing.

"Well, pooh. He sleeps like a dead person."

She leaned over the edge of the tub and tentatively raised her hand, hesitating as she decided where to touch him. Such delicious choices, she mused. No, now, stop. This was serious. He could be a psycho, for all she knew. Maybe she should call the sheriff while her visitor was safely asleep. No, she really didn't feel like explaining why a naked stranger was in her bathtub. Not after the incident with the rooster the week before. It hadn't been *her* fault the rooster had a screwy internal clock and had crowed at two in the morning. No, no sheriff. He wasn't too fond of Cassidy Cole at the moment.

"Okay, here goes," Cassidy said, coaching herself. "I'm waking him up now. Oh, Lord."

She pointed one finger, hesitated again, then picked her spot: the end of the man's nose.

It happened very quickly.

No sooner had Cassidy placed her fingertip squarely on the end of that straight, tanned nose, when a large hand shot out of the water and latched onto her wrist with a viselike grip.

"Aaagh!" Cassidy screamed as she nearly toppled into the water. She sank to her knees by the edge of the tub, and found herself staring into the darkest eyes she'd ever seen; eyes so dark that the pupils were barely discernible. Eyes framed in long lashes a woman would kill to have. Absolutely beautiful eyes. "Hi, there," she said dreamily. "No! Wrong," she added an instant later. "What I meant to say was, who do you think you are, sitting here in my bathtub without so much as a by-your-leave?"

"A what?" the man asked foggily. "A by-your-who?"

Oh, say, now, Cassidy thought, *that* was a voice. Rich, deep, rumbly, sexy as all get-out. What this guy lacked in knees, he certainly made up for in every other area. Outstanding. He was also breaking her wrist.

"Let go of me," she said, pulling on her hand.

He lightened his grip, but not enough for Cassidy to pull free. And then he smiled. He smiled a breath-catching, spread-across-his-face smile that caused Cassidy's heart to do a strange little tap dance. It was a smile that reached the dark, dark pools of his eyes, caused crinkly lines to appear at their corners, and revealed straight white teeth between those kissin' lips. She was sure she was going to faint dead away, fall into the tub and drown. But, oh, saints above, what a way to go!

"I said," she repeated, "let go of my wrist."

"No, I can't do that," he said, the smile slowly fading. Cassidy bid it a fond farewell.

"Why not?"

"Because you might *punch* me in the nose next time. I figure you were checking out my nose to see how much of a wallop it would take to bust it."

"Don't be ridiculous. I was only trying to wake you up to tell you to get out of my bathtub. Which brings us to the subject at hand. Why *are* you in my bathtub? Who are you? How did you get into my apartment? And who do you think you are, helping yourself to my Nightly Sins?"

"Your what?" he asked, his eyes widening.

"Forget that part. Listen, I want you out of this tub immediately. Do you understand? That means now, this very instant."

The smile returned in all its magnificent glory. "Right now?" he asked, all innocence. "You want me to stand up, and step out onto that fluffy rug you're on there?"

"Yes." Cassidy paused. "No! First you have to let go of my wrist so I can leave the room."

"No can do. I have to protect my nose, remember? I'll get out of the tub, but I'm keeping your cute little fist safely away from my cute little nose." He shifted position and started to get up.

"Don't you move!" Cassidy shrieked.

"Whatever," he said, and sank back down. "Do note, though, that the bubbles are fading fast. Things are going to get interesting in a few minutes."

"Oh, dear," Cassidy said, sweeping her gaze over the bubbles, then back to his face.

"We need to negotiate. You want me out of your bathtub. Check. I don't want a broken nose. Check. I could probably figure this out in a flash under normal circumstances, but I'm suffering from a terrible case of jet lag. My brain is a little mushy, you know what I mean? As for my body, I'm turning into a wrinkled prune. I really wish you'd let me get out of this tub. Unless, of course, you're waiting for the free show that's going to take place when all these bubbles disappear."

Cassidy pursed her lips, narrowed her eyes, and glared at him.

Uh-oh, he thought, she was getting mad as hell. Lord, she was something. This was one beautiful woman. Her eyes were as blue as the western sky, her skin was lightly tanned, and, merciful heaven, those lips. She had the most sensuous, kissable lips he'd ever seen. Her hair was a mystery. It was blond, twisted into a lopsided braid on the top of her head. How long was that hair? How would it feel sliding through his fingers, and over his body? Interesting, interesting thought. She wasn't very tall—five foot four, maybe, and proportioned like a dream; small breasts, gently sloping hips; shapely legs in tight, very tight, jeans. Oh, yeah, she was something, all right.

Cassidy took a deep breath, then let it out slowly in an attempt to control her rising temper.

"Look, Mr. . . ." she started. "That's a good place to start. What's your name?"

"Jones."

"Oh, give me a break," she said, rolling her eyes.

"It is! My name has been Jones for thirty-one years. That's because I'm thirty-one years old, which is about ten years older than you are."

"It is not," she said indignantly. "I'm twenty-four. I always look younger when I'm being held captive on the floor of my own bathroom."

He smiled. "Oh, I see."

"What you don't see is that I've had enough of this. I'm calling the sheriff, buster. If he's still ticked off about the rooster, that's too darn bad. I'm a taxpaying citizen, and sheriffs aren't supposed to hold grudges. I'm having you hauled out of here, Mr. Phony Jones."

"Sagan."

"Pardon me?"

"My name isn't Phony Jones, it's Sagan Jones. What rooster?"

"It was hobbling along the sidewalk because it had a sore toe, so I brought it home and—"

"I didn't know roosters had toes," Sagan interrupted.

"Sure, they do. Sort of. Anyway, I was nursing it back to health, but the dumb bird insisted on crowing his little heart out every morning at two o'clock. He never missed. At two A.M. he just cut loose. The neighbors weren't too pleased, and after a week of it someone called the sheriff. I had to drive all the way to Jasper to find it a home on a farm, because everyone around here had heard about his lousy reputation. Have you ever driven all the way to Jasper with a rooster with a sore toe?"

"I can't say that I have."

"It's a grim experience. Oh, well. Where was I?"

Looking more beautiful by the minute, Sagan mused, that was where she was. Lord, she had expressive eyes. And those lips were driving him right out of his mind. Jet lag. Yeah, it was jet lag that was causing his overreaction to her. He could feel it, that hot coil of desire deep in his belly. It was spreading through him. Fast.

"You were going to call the sheriff," he reminded her.

"And I intend to do just that, unless you have some very reasonable answers to my very reasonable questions."

"Fire away," he said pleasantly.

"Why are you in my bathtub?" she yelled. He flinched. "How did you get into my apartment? Just who in blazes are you?"

"Got it," he said, nodding. "I'll rush right through this dissertation, okay? The bubbles are fading fast."

Cassidy's gaze swept over the water again. "Good idea. Hurry up."

"All right. I'm in your bathtub because I've been three days and nights in grungy airports and puddle-jumper planes trying to get back to civilization, and I was filthy. I'm in your apartment because I picked your lock. And I'm Sagan Jones, but we already covered that. There."

"Why me? Why my bathtub? Why my apartment? What did I do to deserve this?"

"Oh, *that* part," Sagan said. "Beaver asked me to check up on you, see if you were doing all right. I hope you appreciate this. Cherokee, Arizona, isn't exactly on the main drag, you know. The plane I flew in to get to the other side of that mountain range was held together by spit and a prayer."

"Beaver sent you?" Cassidy asked, her eyes widening. "My brother?"

"You know more than one person named Beaver?"

"How do I know you know Beaver?"

"I work with him on an oil-drilling site in a classified area, which is why you write to him through a New York APO. He's thirty, blond, six foot two or three, and built like a Sherman tank. The name Beaver fits him because he has this insane habit of chewing on pencils whenever he's doing his heavy thinking. And you are his baby sister, Cassidy. Since I was coming back to the States, he asked me to drop by and see if you needed anything."

"Oh," she said weakly.

"So tell me, Cassidy"—his voice was low and rumbly, and he leaned closer to her—"do you . . . need . . . anything?"

Oxygen, Cassidy thought wildly. She needed oxygen, because the air had rushed from her lungs. What Sagan Jones could do with that voice and those eyes was a sin, it really was.

"Do you?" he repeated, his lips so close to hers, she could feel the flutter of his warm breath.

"Oh, well, I . . . um . . ." Cassidy started dreamily. She blinked. "Yes! I need you out of my bathtub, Sagan Jones." She tugged on her arm and nearly toppled over backward when Sagan released his grip on her. Scrambling to her feet, she yanked a towel from beneath the vanity, and tossed it onto the floor. "There. Out. Now. I'll wait for you in the living room. And hurry up."

"Yes, ma'am," he said with a wicked grin. "Anything you say, ma'am."

Cassidy shot him one more stony glance, stomped out of the bathroom, and slammed the door behind her. But she couldn't shut out the sound of Sagan Jones's laughter. It was, without a doubt, the sexiest sound she'd ever heard, and set off a tingling sensation all along her spine.

In the living room she resisted the urge to pace back and forth, knowing that if she did she would probably trample half of Mrs. Henderson's plants. But, oh, mercy, she was furious. Beaver Cole hadn't sent Sagan Jones out of a sense of brotherly love. No, sir, not by a long shot.

Cassidy stepped over three plants and went into the kitchen. She'd make a pot of coffee. She had to do something to use up some of her excess energy. Angry energy, mad-as-hell energy, ornery-as-a-rooster-with-a-sore-toe energy. Because Sagan Jones was a spy!

She nodded decisively. "That's just the word I want." A spy sent by her brother, the snoop, who didn't believe that Cassidy had a brain in her head. No one "dropped by" Cherokee, Arizona. Sagan had been sent to check up on Beaver Cole's baby sister. She'd strangle that Beaver. She'd cut off his supply of pencils. When, when, when was he going to get it through his thick skull that she was an adult, a grown woman, perfectly capable of taking care of herself? She loved Beaver, she truly did, and she'd tell him that just before she murdered him.

"Coffee smells great," a deep voice said, causing Cassidy to gasp and spin around.

Oh-h-h, she moaned silently, not fair. Sagan Jones didn't play fair. He'd shaved, and now all of that scrumptious face was revealed to her. His faded cut-off jeans hugged his lean hips and accentuated his powerful legs to the point where his knobby knees didn't matter one whit. The blue chambray shirt strained across his wide shoulders, and he'd folded the sleeves up over his tanned, muscled forearms. Bare feet. Bare feet weren't sexy. Oh, darn. On Sagan Jones, bare feet were sexy.

"Western hospitality," Cassidy said, jerking her gaze back to the coffee maker, "dictates that I offer you refreshment. You're welcome to a cup of coffee before you leave."

Sagan chuckled and came into the small kitchen. Leaning against the counter, he crossed one ankle over the other, then folded his arms loosely on his chest. And he kept smiling. Cassidy glanced at him. She felt a funny flutter in the pit of her stomach, and stared at the coffee maker as though it were the most fascinating thing she'd ever seen.

Why was it, she fumed, that some men had so much blatant virility? Sagan Jones might as well have had "bedroom" stamped in indelible ink on his forehead, in an open invitation to any female dumb enough to take him up on it. She wanted this man out of her house! She reached for two mugs and splashed coffee into them, then peered into the steaming brew.

"What do you take in your bed?" she said, not looking at him.

He nearly choked on a burst of laughter. "What?"

"Cream? Sugar? What?" she asked, frowning at him. "That's a reasonable question."

"Yes, *that* is a reasonable question, and the answer is sugar. As for the other question . . . Well, the same thing goes. I like sweet and hot. Very, very hot." He grinned.

"What other question?"

"Miss Cole, you just asked me what I prefer to take into my bed, and now I've told you."

Cassidy planted her hands on her hips. "I did no such thing! I never said one word about . . . I did?"

"You did," Sagan said, nodding. "Are you conducting a general survey on the subject, or are you specifically interested in *my* sexual preferences? I'm not the type to kiss and tell, but"—he shrugged—"in the name of scientific research, I'll be glad to help out. Exactly what do you want to know?"

Cassidy picked up the sugar bowl and shoved it at him. "Put a cork in it, Sagan Jones. This discussion is over." She snatched up her mug and left the kitchen, barely remembering to step over, not on, the plants as she crossed the living room.

Sagan followed, sipping his coffee and glancing around the small apartment. "You have a thing for plants, huh?"

"I'm baby-sitting them for a neighbor," Cassidy said sullenly. She sank onto the sofa.

"Oh. This is an interesting apartment. The building's adobe, isn't it?"

"Yes."

"It seems more like a little house than an apartment, except that it's attached to the others. The complex is built in a square, isn't it?"

"Yes, there's a grassy courtyard in the center. All the back doors open onto it from the dozen apartments. I really like this place, and . . . Why am I talking like this to you?"

Sagan sat down on the opposite end of the sofa. "Because I'm your guest. You're supposed to chat with guests."

"You're not a guest, you're a spy," Cassidy said, narrowing her eyes. "You're a sneaky snoop sent by my meddlesome brother, Clemens Beaver Cole."

"Clemens?" Sagan hooted with laughter. "That's his name? Lord, that's rich. He swears your parents are so weird that they christened him Beaver, and he claims that's what's on his birth certificate."

"Pshaw," she scoffed. "Our parents are unusual, but his name is Clemens. Actually, our folks are dear, wonderful people. They exist in their own space, that's all. I think they're backpacking in the Rocky Mountains at the moment, but I'm not sure. They came to visit me here last year, and were delighted with Cherokee and my lifestyle."

"I think that's what got Beaver so uptight. He said that if your parents approved, you were headed for trouble."

"That's ridiculous. Beaver's a fussbudget. He drives me nuts. I've been in Cherokee a little over a year, and I'm perfectly okay—content and happy. Beaver's a fine one to talk—off doing his secret oil-drilling stuff for the government, and can't even tell me where he is. At least he knows where I am."

"Yeah," Sagan said, glancing around again, "in an adobe house in a town with, what, maybe five thousand people? You're literally cut off from civilization by the mountain range. Plus, Beaver is concerned about this business venture of yours. He said you used your inheritance from your grandmother to buy a bar when you came here."

"It's not a bar. It's a club. Illusions is a club, a fun place to spend the evening."

"Mmm," Sagan said, taking a sip of coffee.

"What is that supposed to mean?"

He shrugged. "Nothing. Beaver mentioned, however, that your family home, a very large, plush home, is sitting empty in San Francisco. He said you could be living there."

"I could. But I choose not to. Beaver and I grew up in that house, mostly under the care of housekeepers, while our parents went off on gold digs, African safaris, whatever. I attended college, got a degree in business management, and set out to find my own niche. I did. Here in Cherokee. And they say women gossip. Is there anything Beaver didn't tell you about me?"

"Lots of things." Sagan set his mug on the end table and got to his feet. "He didn't mention if there was a special man in your life. He showed me your high-school-graduation picture, but failed to tell me that you're now a mature, beautiful, very beautiful, woman. A brother doesn't consider the possibility, I guess, that another man might look at his sister and wonder what her hair would look like brushed free. But *I'm* wondering about that, Cassidy Cole. Oh, yes, I certainly am." He looked directly at her. "I'm thinking about your hair, and about the fact that you have the most kissable-looking lips I've ever seen."

Merciful saints, Cassidy thought wildly, she was going to faint. Sagan's voice, Sagan's eyes, Sagan's body, should be declared illegal. Kissin' lips? She, Cassidy Cole, had kissin' lips? Just as Aunt Patty had said? Really? Fancy that. Oh, she did not. She knew Sagan Jones's type, smooth-talking hustler that he was.

"Mmm," she replied, trying to sound cool and collected.

Sagan chuckled and turned away. "I like the way you've decorated in here. The pottery, Indian rugs on the walls, wicker furniture . . . Nice."

Oh, darn, Cassidy thought, she'd sort of been hoping he'd give her more of that phony-baloney stuff about how luscious she was. She knew it was all a bunch of bull, but once in a while it didn't hurt to hear a sexy man with a sexy voice say things like that. It did wonders for a woman's morale. Oh, well.

"I'm glad you approve of my decorating," she said. "You can report back to Beaver that my apartment scored very high. Well, Mr. Jones"—she got to her feet—"it was nice of you to drop by. Give Beaver my love, and tell him to mind his own business. I'll see you to the door."

"Is that a hint?" Sagan asked with a smile.

"No. The bum's rush is closer to the mark. I hate to be rude, Mr. Jones, but you did come here unannounced, and I'm afraid I have things to do. Have a pleasant trip." She started for the door.

With one powerful step he moved in front of her, trapping her between himself and a potted palm. He was so close, she had to tip her head back to look up at him. He didn't, she noted absently, smell like Nightly Sins bath crystals. His aroma was soapy-fresh and incredibly male. He shoved his hands into the back pockets of his jeans, causing his shirt to strain across his shoulders and chest.

Big macho deal, she thought. The warm flush she could feel on her cheeks didn't mean diddly squat.

"Tally-ho," she said, smiling brightly.

Sagan frowned slightly. "You see, I have a small problem. I can't leave yet."

"Why on earth not?"

"I only have that one piece of carry-on luggage with me. The rest of my things are being shipped. Here."

"What!"

"It was the only way I could do it. I was on puddle-jumper planes, remember? I needed an address to use so the rest of my things could catch up with me."

"Why didn't you use your own address?"

"I don't have one," he said quietly.

"You don't? I mean, what about your family? Isn't there anyone?"

"No."

"I see. Well, that does complicate things a bit, doesn't it? When do you think your things will arrive?"

"Beats me," he said with a shrug.

"I know." Cassidy pointed a finger in the air. "I'll forward it all to you. Good idea? Sure. Just tell me where you're headed, and I'll zip that stuff right to you. How's that?"

"Won't work."

"Why not?"

"Because I don't know where I'm going. No, the best thing to do is just wait here in Cherokee until my things arrive."

"Mr. Jones—"

"Sagan."

"Whatever. When you came into town on the bus, which is the only way to get here from the airport in Jasper, did you notice that there aren't any motels in Cherokee? The people here are farmers, artists, retired folks. A lot work in the copper mines, others in the pecan orchards. We don't get a lot of tourists, so there's no reason to have a motel."

"*You* found a place to live."

"Well, yes, there are a few apartments and little cottages, but it doesn't make much sense to pay for utilities to be turned on, just to be here a few days to wait for your luggage."

Sagan nodded. "Good point. And, I suppose, in a small town like this, everyone knows everyone else's business. You know, they gossip."

"Well, they're aware of what's going on and send the news along, but people don't pass judgment. There's acceptance here in Cherokee, Mr. Jones. I don't know quite how to explain it, but once people cross that mountain range they can leave everything behind. We live by the code of the old West here. If what you are, or what you do, doesn't hurt anyone, no one looks down his nose at you."

"That's nice, very nice. It also solves my problem." Sagan flashed her a hundred-watt smile.

"It does?"

"Sure. I'll stay here with you while I'm waiting for my stuff to catch up with me. I'll sleep on your sofa."

"What?"

"Hey, you gave refuge to a jungle of plants and a rooster with a sore toe. Surely you wouldn't turn

away a weary traveler. What happened to the Western code? 'Mi casa es su casa'?"

"That's in Mexico, I think," Cassidy said absently.

"Fact remains that this is the perfect solution. I
wouldn't do anything to harm your reputation, but
since you've explained the wonderful, open-minded
attitudes of the fine folks of Cherokee, I can bunk in
here. I'll pay my share, of course. Never let it be said
that Sagan Jones is a freeloader. If you keep frowning like that, Cassidy, you're going to get premature
wrinkles."

"No," she said, shaking her head vigorously. "You
can't stay here."

"Why not?"

Why not? she repeated to herself. Because she'd
never lived under the same roof with a man before
except for her father and Beaver, and they didn't
count. Why not? Because Sagan Jones did tricky
little things to her nervous system with his sexy
body, yummy dark eyes, his rumbly, whiskey voice.
Because she wasn't sure she could handle his raw
virility, his masculinity, his blatant sexuality, that
was why not. Because Sagan Jones scared her to
death!

"You're not frightened of me, are you?" he asked
quietly. "Are you, Cassidy?"

"Don't be absurd," she said, then sniffed indignantly for good measure. "I'm an adult, Sagan Jones.
I'm an independent woman, the half owner of a
successful business. A simple houseguest certainly
isn't going to send me into a tizzy."

"Great. Then it's settled."

"It is? Oh, well, no, I—"

"Deal?" He extended his hand.

She stared at his hand, his face, then his hand again. This was how crazy things always happened to her, she thought dismally. One minute they weren't happening, and in the next . . . shazam . . . she was right smack dab in trouble again. Well, not this time, by gum. She was going to open her mouth and deliver a loud, clear "no" to one Mr. Sagan Jones.

"Cassidy?"

"Yes," she said softly. She watched with detached fascination as her hand lifted and was grasped by Sagan's large, tanned one, his fingers curling around hers.

"Thank you," he said. "I'll be as quiet as a mouse. You won't even know I'm here."

That, Cassidy thought dryly, was the most ridiculous thing she'd ever heard. There was heat radiating from Sagan's hand. Heat that traveled up her arm, shot across her breasts, and sizzled deep inside her. Not know that he was there? She was already all too aware that Sagan Jones was there.

Cassidy drew in a shuddering breath.

Oh, mercy, what had she done?

Two

Sagan lay stretched out on the sofa, his feet hanging over one end, his hands under his head, as he
stared out of the window. He could hear the water
running in the shower as Cassidy prepared to go to
her bar, or club, or whatever she called it.

Darkening shadows crept over the room, but Sagan
didn't want to turn on the lamp. He had a perfect
view of the April Western sunset beyond Cassidy's
windows. The sky was streaked with rich hues of
purple, orange, and yellow, each melting one into
the next like warmed butter. He thoroughly enjoyed
the spectacle of nature until the niggling question
in his brain turned from a nagging whisper to a
shout.

What in the hell did he think he was doing?

Why, he asked himself, had he insisted on staying
on at Cassidy Cole's? Hell, he didn't know. Yes, it
was true that he'd had his belongings shipped to
her address. But he could have left Cherokee, settled

in somewhere, then let Cassidy know where to forward his stuff. He could have been on the rickety bus at that very moment, heading back over the mountains.

But he didn't want to go.

He had no plans, no destination, no one waiting for him. He was back in the United States after ten years of moving from one foreign oil-drilling site to the next. He was home, and nobody gave a damn.

"So?" he said aloud, and ran his hand down his face. Why did it matter? He was a loner, had been since he was sixteen years old. He needed no one, kept his emotions under tight control. Very few men, and no women, had been allowed to really know him. Oh, he'd had his share of women, had discovered early on that his looks and build attracted them. He made no promises, took only what they offered, enjoyed pleasing them in bed. But none of them had mattered.

"Like a damn stud," he muttered. Staying on in Cherokee had nothing to do with Cassidy Cole and her big blue eyes. Her oh, so kissable lips. Or the lush swell of her breasts and sweet slope of her hips. He was well aware of her attributes, but they had nothing to do with his decision to stay. He simply needed to stop for a moment, take a deep breath, and figure out what in hell he was going to do with the rest of his life.

Lord, he was tired, Sagan thought with a sigh. Tired in body, and tired in mind and soul. He needed peace. He needed to be home. But the lousy part was, he didn't have a home to go to. It had never mattered before, but now he felt so damn empty.

Ah, what the hell, he reasoned. He'd stay in Cherokee for a few days, check out Cassidy's bar, her friends, then report to Beaver. Beaver was a good man, a buddy, and it was the decent thing to do.

He nodded in satisfaction, but when Cassidy's voice lilted through the air as she sang a sad country-western song, a tight knot formed in his stomach.

She was a beautiful woman. She even sang like an angel. And those lips. They were enough to send a man over the edge. What would they feel like, taste like, moving beneath his? And when he took her in his arms? Oh, she'd be heaven itself nestled against him, her soft curves meeting his hard body. Her hair. Lord above, he wanted to know the secrets of that hair—how long it was, its fragrance, the feel of it sliding slowly over him.

Hot desire coiled within him, and his heart thudded as he imagined himself removing Cassidy's clothes. She was small, fragile, and he knew he'd be incredibly aware of his own strength when he made love to her. He'd be gentle, assuring her pleasure before his own, before he moved over her and into the honeyed warmth of her body. They would be so good together. So damn good.

"That's all, Jones," he mumbled, swinging his feet to the floor. "Knock it off." Whew, he mused, running his hand over the back of his neck. He'd really gotten carried away. He'd never fantasized that way about a woman before. He'd never had to, because there were always plenty available.

So why was he doing it now? Cassidy Cole wasn't even his type. Gorgeous, yes, but there was an innocence about her, something that made a man want to protect her, stand between her and anything or anyone who might hurt her. Protectiveness was a strange sentiment for him, but he felt it. And he also felt plain, old, honest-to-goodness lust. He wanted Cassidy Cole.

But she was Beaver's sister, he reminded himself sternly.

Sagan's head snapped around when Cassidy's bedroom door opened, and his eyes widened when he saw her. He turned on the lamp to get a better look, opened his mouth to speak, realized that nothing was going to come out, and clamped it shut again.

"Problem?" she asked nonchalantly.

Slowly he rose, his eyes riveted on her. "A clown? You're dressed like a clown?"

"Very good. You figured that out all by yourself."

"Why are you dressed like a clown?"

"Because it's Friday," she said pleasantly.

"Oh," he said, throwing up his hands, "of course. That explains it perfectly."

Cassidy laughed. "The name of the club is Illusions, remember? Each day we create a different illusion. Friday is clown day. Barry and I thought it was very clever, and the customers love it."

"Barry? Who's Barry?"

"Barry Howlett, my partner. We each own half of Illusions. Well, I've got to be going. Help yourself to whatever is in the kitchen."

"Hold it," Sagan said, raising his hand. "How old is this Barry?"

"Thirty-five."

"Mmm."

"I really hate it when you make that noise," she said, and started toward the door.

"Halt!"

She burst into laugher. "Halt? You sound like a sentry."

"Dammit, wait a minute." Sagan strode past her and blocked the door. He looked her over again. "Lord, you look weird. A green-and-yellow clown suit, for cripe's sake."

"Cute, huh? I made it myself. I made all the different costumes. For Barry and the waitresses too." She tried to push past him. "Sagan, I really must be getting to work."

"Do you have something going with Barry?"

"I told you. He's my partner."

"Beyond that," he demanded. "You know, a thing going, a relationship, a—dammit, Cassidy, are you sleeping with that guy?"

She squinted at him. "That's none of your business."

"Ah-ha! That means you are."

"I am not!"

"You're not?" A smile lit his face instantly. "That's good news."

"Why, pray tell, is that good news?"

"Oh, well, because . . . because Beaver might get up-tight if you were sleeping with Barry Whoever."

"That's none of Beaver's concern."

"I'm glad to hear you say that," Sagan said under his breath.

"What?"

"Nothing."

"Would you kindly move your carcass, Mr. Jones? I really have to go."

"Yeah, sure, just as soon as I kiss you."

"I beg your pardon?"

"You see, Cassidy"—he cradled her face between

his hands—"I've never kissed a woman wearing a green-and-yellow clown suit. I think that life should be experienced to the fullest, don't you?"

"I never really"—Cassidy swallowed heavily—"thought about it, I guess."

He lowered his head slowly toward hers. "Think about it." His warm breath fluttered across her lips. "Experiencing life to the fullest." He brushed his lips over hers. "Fantastic."

"Mmm," she murmured as her knees began to tremble.

He kissed the edge of her mouth, then the other edge, and she was sure she was going to die, absolutely die, if he didn't get on with it and really kiss her. Her arms floated upward and circled his neck as he continued to tease, flicking his tongue along her bottom lip.

"Quit messing around, Sagan," she said breathlessly.

A chuckle rumbled up from Sagan's chest. Then he claimed her mouth, and with it, Cassidy was convinced, he also claimed every bit of air she had in her body.

Sagan Jones did, indeed, Cassidy thought dreamily, have kissin' lips.

The moment his lips touched hers, desire ripped through Sagan with a shudder. He slid one hand to the nape of her neck, the other to her back, as he drew her close to him. With gentle insistence he pushed his tongue inside her mouth and explored every secret crevice. Her tongue met his and the heat gathered deep within him, pounding through his veins, causing his manhood to strain against his jeans.

Kissing Cassidy Cole was everything he had imagined. And more. She fit next to him as though she'd been custom-made, just for him, waiting just for him. She tasted so good, and felt so damn good, and, oh, Lord, he wanted to make love to this woman.

He lifted his head, drawing a ragged breath as he trailed nibbling kisses down her slender throat. Then he moved again to take full possession of her mouth in a kiss that was urgent, hungry, hard. A kiss that he never wanted to end.

Cassidy answered Sagan's demands, felt the evidence of his arousal pressing against her. She was swept away in a tide of sensations, savoring each wave as it assaulted her. The rhythm of his stroking tongue was matched by a similar cadence deep within her, in that dark, feminine place that ached with a sweet pain. Crushed against his hard chest, her breasts grew tender, sensitive to his every labored breath.

Never in her entire life had she been kissed like this. Never. Cassidy knew it, and hovered between fear and a glorious sense of being on the brink of a new and wondrous place. Desire thrummed within her, making her acutely aware of every inch of her own body, and aware of the power and strength of the body of the man who held her.

Sagan Jones. His name echoed in her mind as she filled her senses with his taste and aroma, the feel of his steely muscles, the outward evidence of his need that could fulfill the heated ache deep inside her. She trembled in his arms as a hazy mist drifted over her, clouding her last link with reality and reason.

In the far recesses of Sagan's passion-laden mind, he registered the fact that Cassidy had surrendered to him, totally, completely. She was molded against him, soft and pliant. Tiny whimpers of need escaped from her throat. She was his for the taking, and he knew it. He had aroused her with practiced ease, and soon she would tell him how much she wanted him. She would come to him willingly, eagerly, ready to receive all he had to give her. And he would comply. He would whisper close to her lips, ask her if she was certain she wanted this. She would nod, her hands would reach to remove his clothes. Oh, yes, Cassidy Cole was his now. His for the taking.

And he hated himself.

A strange new voice hammered against his brain, taunting him, filling him with guilt and shame. He groaned deeply as he thrust his tongue into Cassidy's mouth, warring against the voice in his head, waiting for his passion to still it. Then he could join his body with Cassidy's and appease the throbbing ache of desire.

Dammit it, his mind screamed. Every inch of her was telling him that she wanted him, and he was going to have her. She was a woman capable of making her own decisions. She was like all those other women, responsible for her own actions and—

No! the voice said. She wasn't just one more in the line of the now-faceless women he had bedded. This was Cassidy. Beautiful Cassidy, with the hint of innocence and vulnerability. Cassidy Cole, who had raised his passion higher than anything he could remember.

And he couldn't have her.

"Oh, hell!"

Sagan gripped Cassidy's shoulders and pushed her away from him, but held on tightly when he felt her sway unsteadily on her feet. She slowly lifted her lashes. He groaned inwardly when he saw the smoky blue of her eyes, the moist, swollen lips that were begging for more kisses, the flush of desire on her cheeks.

"Oh, hell?" Cassidy whispered.

"Yeah," he said gruffly. "Oh, hell. And dammit it. And a lot of other things I could say. Lord, lady, quit looking at me like that, or I'm going to finish what we started here."

"I beg your pardon?" she asked breathlessly.

"Cassidy!"

She came back to earth with a thud. "Oh!" She stepped backward out of his arms, her eyes wide. "Oh, my. Oh, dear me."

"No joke," he said, glaring at her.

"Well, for Pete's sake," she said, matching his expression, "I've heard of kiss-and-tell, but never kiss-and-crabby. What is your problem, Sagan Jones?"

Sagan stared at the ceiling. "I can't believe she actually said that."

Cassidy's gaze dropped below Sagan's waist. "Oh," she said in a small voice.

He pointed a long finger at her. "You are dangerous to yourself. Do you go around kissing all your men the way you kissed me? You're lucky I'm a nice guy"—Oh, what a bunch of bull—"or you'd be flat on your back in bed right now." Soft and willing, holding out her arms to him. Lord. "You need a keeper, Cassidy Cole." She needed a lover. Him. Oh, Jones, shut up.

"I do not," she shot back. "I was completely under control while I was kissing you." Liar, liar, pants on fire. "You have an overblown ego, Mr. Jones. Just because you kiss a woman doesn't mean she's going to start climbing up your body, begging you to take her to bed." Wanna make a bet? "Kisses are kisses. No big deal." Oh, her nose was going to grow all the way across the room and right out of the window.

"Mmm," Sagan said, still glowering at her.

"That's it. I've had it," Cassidy stomped past him to the door. "I'm going to work. Good-bye."

"Cassidy."

The raw sensuality of Sagan's voice when he said her name stopped Cassidy dead in her tracks. She turned slowly to face him.

"Yes?" she asked in a hushed voice.

He closed the distance between them and gently slid his hands to her throat. Looking directly into her eyes, he let his thumbs trace the line of her jaw, then her cheeks.

Those eyes, Cassidy thought frantically. Those damnable dark, fathomless eyes. And oh, mercy, those kissin' lips.

"Kissing you," he said, his voice slightly husky as he trailed one thumb over her lips, "was heaven itself." He leaned toward her, then jerked his head back up. "I'll see you later."

"Later," Cassidy repeated, and hurried out the door.

"See ya, Cassidy Cole," Sagan said quietly to the empty room. He shoved his hands into his back pockets and stared at the closed door. "Ah, hell."

Scowling, Sagan went into the kitchen. He emerged a short time later with three peanut-butter sandwiches and a glass of milk. On the sofa he ate his make-do dinner and stared into space.

Strange, he thought. His entire behavior regarding Cassidy Cole was strange, totally unlike him. He should have been in bed with the woman at that very moment, making sweet, slow, sensuous love. But here he sat, Romeo Extraordinaire, eating peanut-butter sandwiches, with no one to talk to but a bunch of plants.

Why? he asked himself. Why hadn't he made love to Cassidy? Heaven knew he had an ache in his gut for her that ten cold showers wouldn't cure. He'd wanted her—had he ever—and she'd wanted him. Where had that wet blanket of a voice come from, telling him that Cassidy wasn't his to have? Jet lag? The fact that she was Beaver's sister? No, it had been something else, something deep within him that had told him he couldn't have lived with himself if he'd followed through on what he'd set out to do. What a helluva time to discover he had a streak of nobility.

You're a swell human being, Sagan told himself dryly. A top-notch guy, Jones. You deserve points for your sexual restraint. The lousy part was, he still knew he'd done the right thing. Cassidy was different. She was special. Wide-eyed. Innocent.

But there was such passion in that soft, feminine body, even covered by that screwy green-and-yellow clown suit. When Cassidy made love, she'd be fantastic, offer all she was, receive all her man had to give her.

Sagan sat bolt upright, nearly spilling his milk. Man? What man? Barry Whoever? He'd kill him! Some twit who wore a clown suit because it was Friday wasn't good enough for Cassidy. No, sir. Barry Whoever had a news flash coming his way. He'd better keep his clown-suited self away from Cassidy

Cole or he'd answer to Sagan Jones, by damn. Because . . . yes, because Sagan had told Beaver he'd check up on Cassidy, make sure she was doing okay. Well, a pansy in a clown suit wasn't okay for Cassidy. No way.

"Mmm," Sagan said. He'd better get over to that bar. It was, after all, the only way to get all the facts for his buddy Beaver. He'd prefer, of course, just to stay in the apartment and sack out, get some sleep, but duty called. Ah, the sacrifices a man made for a friend.

Smiling, Sagan sank back against the cushions on the sofa and took a large bite of his sandwich.

Illusions was on the edge of town, in what had once been a carriage house. It had a distinctly western feel—airy and open, with a wood-beamed ceiling and a long, highly polished bar. Rough-cut tables and chairs circled a dance floor. Four young men who worked in the copper mine by day played western music, and a jukebox against one wall took over when the band had a break.

The atmosphere was friendly, noisy, and relaxed. The lighting was dim enough to hide the nicks and scars in the old tables, but not so dark that there might be "hanky-panky" in the corners. Women were as welcome as men, if anyone got drunk he was relieved of his car keys and hauled home by friends, and pinching a waitress got a customer banned for a solid week. The clientele ranged in age from just turned legal to senior citizens, and a good time was had by all.

By the time Cassidy arrived at the club, the Friday-night crowd was already thick. Barry, decked out in his clown suit, was making drinks behind the bar. Carmen and Mitzy, the two clown-suited waitresses, were scurrying around serving customers.

"Sorry I'm late," Cassidy said to Barry as she scooted behind the bar.

"No problem," he told her.

"How's Barbie?"

"Not so good, Cassidy. I need to talk to you later."

"What's wrong? Barbie's all right, isn't she? And the baby? I know Barbie's eager to have this pregnancy over with, but everything is okay, isn't it? Barry?"

He frowned. "Later, Cassidy. It's too complicated to explain right now. Wait until the band starts playing and there's a lull. I need a batch of Margaritas."

"I'll make them," she offered. She stared at him for a long moment in search of a clue as to what was wrong, but found none. With a frown she turned to reach for the tequila.

For the next hour Cassidy was busy making drinks and delivering them to the boisterous crowd. She greeted everyone by name, received shouts of hello in return, and moved with speed and efficiency.

She also thought about Sagan Jones.

Much to her annoyance, thoughts of Sagan were never far from her mind. She could see him as clearly as though he were standing before her. If she shut her eyes for even a brief second, she could relive with crystal clarity the taste of his mouth on hers, his aroma, the feel of his steely muscles, and her own wondrous yearnings.

Sagan Jones was, in short, driving her crazy!

When a round of applause went up from the throng, Cassidy knew the band had arrived. She blew the musicians a kiss, then hurried behind the bar to talk to Barry.

"Barry," she said anxiously, "what's wrong with Barbie?"

He ran his fingertips over his forehead, which did nothing to diminish the frown lines there. "The doctor is worried about her," he said. "She's showing signs of toxemia. Her feet have been swelling for a few weeks, but he wasn't too concerned. Now he doesn't like the looks of things. The baby is due in a month, you know. The doc wants to put Barbie in the hospital in Jasper so that he can monitor her for a while."

"She must be scared to death. Oh, you poor things. When are you leaving?"

"That's just it, Cassidy. I don't know what to do. I'm supposed to check her into the hospital tomorrow, and Barbie is so frightened. I want to stay in Jasper with her, but—"

"Of course you'll stay with her," Cassidy said. "That's where you belong."

"But what about you and Illusions? I have responsibilities here."

"Pshaw. That's the beauty of having your own business. I'll handle things here, Barry. You trust me to do a good job, don't you?"

"Of course I do. You're my partner. But you see, Cassidy, I'm not sure how long I'll be gone."

"Worry not, sweetheart. I'll make our first million while you're in Jasper. You concentrate on Barbie and that baby, leave tomorrow on schedule, and tell Barbie I love her to pieces."

Barry threw his arms around Cassidy and hugged her. "Thank you, dear friend."

At the exact moment that Barry Howlett was hugging Cassidy, Sagan walked in the door of Illusions.

"I knew it," he muttered. "That six-foot pansy is dead meat." He strode to the bar and smacked his palm on the shiny surface, causing Cassidy and Barry to jerk apart. "Beer," Sagan said, his dark eyes riveted on Barry. "Any brand."

"Sagan," Cassidy said. "What are you doing here?"

Barry set a bottle in front of Sagan. "You know this guy, Cassidy?"

"She's living with this guy," Sagan said, his voice low and cold.

Cassidy's eyes widened. "What? I am not. How dare you say such a thing, Sagan Jones."

"Okay." He shrugged. "I'll rephrase it. *I'm* living with *you*."

"You are not!"

He flashed her a dazzling smile. "Sure, I am darlin'. We discussed it, remember? Right after the little chat we had in the bathroom while you were watching me take my bath."

Cassidy glanced quickly at Barry, then leaned across the bar to glare at Sagan.

"You hush your mouth, Sagan Jones." She was close to punching him in the nose.

"Hello, hello, hello," a voice sang out.

"Oh, dear Lord, not Aunt Patty." Cassidy groaned. "Not now."

"Hi, Aunt Patty," Barry said. "The usual?"

"You betcha, sonny boy. Cherry Coke straight up, with two cherries," said the pint-sized woman. "I'll run a tab." She looked at Sagan. "Here's a new face in Cherokee." Her gaze traveled over him slowly. "Say, there, you do know how to fill out a pair of jeans, you handsome devil, you."

Sagan chuckled. "Thank you, ma'am."

"Oh, and he's got manners to boot," Aunt Patty said. "Muscles, too, and kissin' lips. Whatcha doing in Cherokee, good-looking?"

"I'm living with Cassidy, ma'am," Sagan said pleasantly.

"Oh-h-h," Cassidy moaned, covering her face with her hands. "I'm going to strangle him."

"Why didn't you tell me you were living with a man, Cassidy?" Barry asked. "I realize it's none of my business, but—"

"Damn right, it isn't . . . clown," Sagan said, his tone dark and fierce. "I think you and I need to have a little chat."

"Hot damn," Aunt Patty said merrily, "he's macho, too. You did yourself up proud here, Cassidy. Good for you."

"Good for Cassidy?" Carmen asked, coming up to the group. "What did she do?"

"Nothing," Cassidy replied. "Absolutely nothing."

"She snagged this gorgeous hunk of man," Aunt Patty said. "Feast your eyes on this specimen, Carmen."

"Oh, good Lord." Sagan growled into his beer.

"Nice, nice, nice." Carmen nodded her approval as she scrutinized Sagan. "Mitzy," she called, "come over here and see what Cassidy found."

"Dammit, Cassidy," Sagan said, "would you call these people off?"

Cassidy examined her fingernails. "You started it, Sagan."

"Well, what do you expect?" he roared. "I walked in here and found this . . . overgrown stuffed toy with his hands all over you."

"Barry was giving me a hug. Besides, it's none of your business."

Sagan started to protest. "It sure as hell *is* my business, because . . ." Because why? He'd felt the fury explode within him when he saw Cassidy in the creepy clown's arms. And that was because . . . There was a logical reason for his reaction, but he couldn't quite get a handle on it. It was . . . "Beaver. Yes, that's it. Your brother wouldn't like it."

"Brother, my big toe," Aunt Patty said. "You're jealous as all get-out, young man, which stands to reason, since you're living with Cassidy."

Sagan scoffed. "Jealous? Me? Don't be silly. I don't have a jealous bone in my body, ma'am."

"Call me Aunt Patty, cutie. The whole town does."

"You've got plenty of other good stuff going in that body," freckle-faced Mitzy said, deciding to get her two-cents' worth in.

"Don't bother to wiggle your cute little fanny in front of him, Mitzy," Aunt Patty said. "He belongs to Cassidy."

"He does not," Cassidy said.

"You don't?" Mitzy asked Sagan.

"I'm living with her."

"Here we go again," Cassidy said, throwing up her hands. "I've had enough of this nonsense. Everyone listen up. This man is Sagan Jones, who is a friend of my brother's. Mr. Jones is sleeping on my sofa while waiting for his luggage to catch up with him. Then he's leaving. That's it. End of story."

"Bull," Aunt Patty said.

"Boring," Carmen said.

Barry spoke up. "Hey, look, Sagan, I think you got the wrong impression of what was happening between Cassidy and me when you walked in."

"I know what I saw." Sagan drained his beer bottle.

"What you saw," Barry said, "was me hugging my dear friend for being so understanding about my having to leave her here alone to tend to Illusions. The doctor says my pregnant wife has to check into the hospital in Jasper for observation, and I want to be with her."

"Wife?" Sagan asked weakly.

"Wife," Cassidy repeated.

"Oh." Sagan paused. "Oh, I see. Well, I . . . um . . . I'll have another beer."

"Is Barbie going to be all right?" Aunt Patty asked.

"I hope so," Barry said quietly. "We're really scared for the baby, Aunt Patty."

"Shoot, boy, they'll be fine. Barbie and that baby will be right as rain."

"I really do hope so. In the meantime, I'm leaving Cassidy shorthanded here. Did you ever tend bar, Aunt Patty?"

"Nope," she said. "Tried a lot of things in my day, but bartending wasn't one of them. Surely someone around here knows how to mix up all that fancy stuff."

"*I* do," Sagan said.

Aunt Patty beamed at him. "The man just doesn't quit. Oh, I do like you, Sagan Jones."

"Ditto," Carmen put in. "Oops. My fans call. Mitzy, you take Harley's table. I'll get Chunky and his crew."

"Okay," Mitzy said. "It was nice meeting you, Sagan. I hope you enjoy living with Cassidy."

"He's not—" Cassidy started to say.

"I'm sure I will," Sagan interrupted. "See you later, Mitzy."

"I'm off to hear the band," Aunt Patty said. "That Ricky, who plays lead guitar, is a sexy son-of-a-gun, isn't he? I don't know how he breathes with his jeans that tight. Keep us posted on Barbie, Barry. Sure glad you popped into Cherokee, Sagan."

"Thank you, ma'am . . . I mean, Aunt Patty," he answered with a smile.

"Kissin' lips," Aunt Patty muttered as she scurried away. "That man has the most kissin' lips I ever did see."

Cassidy smiled. Amen to that, she thought. Sagan was pushy, arrogant, and butted his nose in where it didn't belong. But oh, yes, he did have kissin' lips.

"Well!" Barry said, snapping Cassidy back to attention. "It seems you have a bartender to help you while I'm gone, Cassidy. That's terrific. It'll ease my conscience while I'm in Jasper."

"Glad to help out," Sagan said pleasantly.

"Cassidy is a first-rate bartender herself," Barry went on. "If you know your stuff, Sagan, you two will be fine here."

"Oh, I know my stuff." Sagan looked directly at Cassidy. "Don't you agree, Cassidy? Don't you think I know my stuff?"

"I've never seen you tend bar, Mr. Jones," she said stiffly. He wasn't talking about bar stuff, the louse.

Sagan gave her a lazy smile. "Mmm." He wasn't referring to making drinks, and the flush on Cassidy's cheeks said she knew it. Lord, she was a beautiful woman. "Guess I'll have to prove myself, then. Right, Cassidy?"

Cassidy glared at him.

"You bet," Barry put in. He looked at the stormy expression on Cassidy's face, then at the grin on Sagan's. "And there's no time like the present. I'll go help Carmen and Mitzy wait tables. Sagan, come on back here and start figuring out where we keep everything. Good idea? Yep." He inched around Cassidy and out from behind the bar. "See ya."

Sagan chuckled, got slowly to his feet, and came around the bar to stand beside Cassidy. He looked over the supply of liquor and sparkling glasses. "Nice setup."

"Don't speak to me." Cassidy stared straight ahead. "Do not say one word to me, Sagan Jones. I have never been so furious in my entire life. How dare you come in here and . . . Oh, don't get me started. I'll use up all my oxygen."

"You're low on lemon slices," Sagan said. "Want me to fill that little dish?"

Cassidy spun around to face him, eyes narrowed, lips pursed together.

Sagan hooted with laughter. "I know where the lemon slices went. You ate them. Clowns are supposed to smile, darlin'. Hey, is that any way to treat a guy who's offered to bail you out of a rough spot? I could get all in a snit and leave, you know. Better be nice to me, Miss Cole. You need me."

Cassidy opened her mouth to retort.

Sagan stepped closer to her and trailed his thumb lightly over her cheek, his smile gone, his obsidian eyes locking into Cassidy's blue ones.

"Don't you?" he asked in a low voice. "Don't you need me, Cassidy?"

To do what? Cassidy wondered dreamily. Kiss her? Hold her? Wrap those steely arms around her and pull her next to that rock-hard body? Oh, you'd better believe it, Sagan.

"Cassidy," Carmen said, zooming up to the bar.

Cassidy jerked away in surprise. "You scared me to death, Carmen."

"I work here, remember?" Carmen said frowning. "Listen, Jerry is here with his wife, and it's her birthday. He wants to buy her a brandy Manhattan. No one ever ordered a brandy Manhattan before. Can you make one?"

"Hold it." Sagan made a quick check of the bar supplies. "Yep, no sweat. I have everything I need. One brandy Manhattan coming right up, Carmen."

"I'm impressed," the attractive waitress said.

Sagan reached for a bottle. "I do know my stuff. All I have to do is convince Cassidy of that."

"Mmm," Cassidy said, folding her arms over her breasts. "Just . . . mmm."

Three

At one A.M. the boisterous crowd made its exit from Illusions. People shouted their farewells, yelled that they'd return the next night. A few even praised Sagan for his fine job of bartending. Cassidy smiled, and waved to her customers, and Sagan nodded pleasantly. She shooed Barry out with the others, so he could get a decent night's sleep before driving Barbie to Jasper the next day.

And then it was quiet in Illusions. Very, very quiet. There was no sound except for the occasional squeak of a clean cloth on the glasses that Sagan was polishing to a sparkling shine.

Cassidy looked at Sagan from beneath her lashes, only to find that he was concentrating on his task. His face was unreadable. It gave no clue as to what he was thinking.

Her gaze flickered over him, and she was struck once again by the raw masculinity, the blatant sexuality, he exuded. Each part of his tightly muscled body was perfectly beautiful. She had seen the appreciative looks the other women had given him that night, and the dazzling, heart-stopping smiles he'd given back to them all, old and young alike. The men, too, had liked Sagan. They recognized and appreciated that his physique had come from hard labor, not workouts at a fancy health club. They'd soon counted him as one among them, no questions asked.

Sagan Jones had come, seen, and conquered Cherokee, Arizona.

Cassidy grabbed a wet cloth and walked from behind the bar to wipe off the tables. She pushed in the chairs with more force than was necessary, and realized to her own annoyance that she was angry at Sagan.

Darn him, she fumed. He just zoomed into town, flexed his muscles, smiled that killer smile with his kissin' lips, and had the populace eating out of his hand. He'd announced, like an arrogant so-and-so, that he was living with her, and everyone thought that was just hunky-dory. Didn't anyone care or worry about *her*? About what kind of trouble she might be getting into by taking this stranger into her home? This was *her* town, not Sagan's. Where was her friends' loyalty?

Brother, Cassidy thought, she sounded like a pouting six-year-old. Of course her friends hadn't questioned or passed judgment on Sagan's arrival or his living arrangements. This was Cherokee, and the "live and let live" philosophy was one of its most endearing qualities.

Cassidy shoved another chair into place. One thing was for sure, she admitted. Sagan was one heck of a bartender. He was fast and efficient, and when Chunky and crew had decided to test out fancy drinks they'd never had before, Sagan had prepared them all with expertise. He could carry on a conversation and never lose track of what he was doing. Sagan Jones did indeed know his stuff. But how had an oil driller become such a skillful bartender? she wondered.

As she vigorously wiped a sticky table, more questions flitted through her mind. Sagan had said he had no one to ship his belongings to. No one? No family at all? How strange. And how sad. Belongings? Everything? Was he quitting his job as an oil driller? Why? He'd said he didn't know where he was going, had no plans. Why not? Lord above, who and what was Sagan Jones? Granted, he knew Beaver, but still . . . What did she really know about this man, this drifter?

Well, she thought, he kissed like a dream, that much she knew. Oh, shame on her. He could be an ax murderer, for all she knew, and he was sleeping on her sofa! Oh, cripes, how did she get herself into these messes?

Cassidy glanced up as Sagan walked past her to the jukebox. He surveyed the selection, dropped in several coins, then pushed some buttons. Moments later a sad, dreamy western song drifted through the air, filling the silence with the tale of a lost love and a broken heart.

Sagan turned and extended his hand to Cassidy.

Again, there was no readable expression on his face, but Cassidy felt her heart begin to race. She dropped the cloth onto the table, then ran her hands over the clown suit to dry them, her gaze never leaving the dark pools of Sagan's eyes.

Yes? No? she asked herself. Should she dance with him? There, alone, in the dimly lit atmosphere of Illusions? Just the two of them, with Sagan holding her in his powerful arms? Maybe it wasn't a very good idea. The kisses shared with Sagan in her living room had proven her susceptibility to his magnetism. No, she wouldn't dance with him.

Cassidy walked slowly across the room and into Sagan's arms.

Ecstasy.

And heat. Strong, strong arms holding her tightly against a rock-hard body that fit next to hers with exacting perfection. Oh, yes, she thought dreamily, this was ecstasy. For the life of her she couldn't remember moving across the dance floor and into Sagan's embrace. But now she was there, and there was nowhere, *nowhere* else she wished to be. Sagan danced with smooth, athletic grace, and she was convinced that if he loosened his hold on her, she'd either dissolve into a heap at his feet or float away into oblivion.

The music played on.

Sagan tightened his hold on Cassidy, and felt her soft breasts crushed against his chest. He filled his senses with her fresh, feminine aroma, and resisted the urge to pull the pins from her hair so he could see it tumble free.

She felt so good in his arms, he thought. Felt good, and smelled good, and if he lifted her head up and kissed her, she would taste good too. Asinine green-and-yellow clown suit or no, Cassidy Cole was the most desirable woman he had ever met.

A soft purr of pleasure rose from Cassidy's throat, causing a heated coil of need to throb deep within him. His manhood stirred, and blood pounded in his veins. He brushed his lips over her forehead, then kissed the eyelids that had drifted closed. He tilted his head down at the exact moment when she moved hers back, and claimed her mouth, his tongue delving into the sweet darkness.

And they continued to dance.

The song ended, another started, and the kiss went on and on. Sagan's hands dropped to Cassidy's back; hers lifted to his neck. They swayed to the music, their tongues meeting, keeping rhythm with the seductive melody.

Senses meshed, heat, and aromas, and awareness of a body hard, a body soft. Currents of sexuality seemed to weave around and through them, holding them close together with invisible, unbreakable threads.

Cassidy could feel Sagan's arousal pressing against her; full, strong, promising so much, so very much. Desire thrummed within her, causing her heart to race and a flush to stain her cheeks. Never before had she felt so feminine, so womanly, so filled with the need and want for a man, this man, this Sagan Jones. Without even realizing it, she had been waiting for Sagan to come into her life, and now he was there. And he wanted her. His body spoke boldly of his need, matching the passion that churned unchecked throughout her. She didn't have to question the right or wrong of her need, for this was Sagan, and this was ecstasy.

Sagan tore his mouth from Cassidy's to draw a ragged breath, then blazed a trail of fiery kisses down her slender throat. She tilted her head back further, exposing more of her soft skin to him, her labored breathing echoing his own. His hands roamed restlessly over her back, then down to the slope of her buttocks, fitting her to him as he moved to the music. The steady beat of the song matched the hot pulsing deep within her as he pressed her even closer to the evidence of all that declared him to be man.

"Oh, Sagan." Her whisper was hardly more than a passion-laden sound.

Sagan felt her tremble in his arms, felt the taut buds of her breasts heavy against his chest, felt her surrender as she molded herself to his aching body.

"I want you, Cassidy," he murmured. "I want to be inside you, feel your silken heat tighten around me. We're going to fly away together, and it's going to be so damn good. Let me love you, here, at Illusions, where we'll create our own illusion. There's no world beyond this place, this moment. It's ours. You'll be my illusion, and I'll be yours."

Cassidy drifted back from a hazy place, confusion causing a slight frown to shadow her features. Illusion? her mind repeated. But illusions weren't real, they were make-believe, like being a clown because it was Friday. To become someone's lover because . . . simply because they were there . . . to create an illusion instead of a special meaning, to share such intimacy with a man, then have the illusion change back into reality, as all illusions did . . . was wrong. Very, very wrong.

Cassidy stiffened in Sagan's arms.

And the music stopped.

"What is it, Cassidy?" He pulled her closer to him.

"I . . . No," she said, shaking her head. She tried to step away from him, only to feel the steel bands of his arms tighten even more. "Oh, Lord, what have I done?"

"Nothing . . . yet," he said, his voice gritty with passion. "Cassidy, I want you, and you want me. There's nothing wrong with that. It's real, honest."

"No, it would be an illusion, just as you said. An illusion isn't real, Sagan. It's something that appears for a fleeting moment. Then it's forgotten."

"It wouldn't be like that. Our being together, making love, would be special, hold special meaning for both of us." Ah, damn, he fumed inwardly. Listen to him. He was pleading his case like a kid in the backseat of a car. What in the hell was the matter with him? It was as though the emptiness, the loneliness, within him were turning into a gnawing, painful hunger; a hunger to belong, care, share, have it matter to someone if he lived or died. Have it matter to Cassidy. Physically he wanted her, ached for her, but it was more than that, much more. Or was it all just an illusion created by the music, the hour, the place, the woman herself? Dammit, he didn't know.

"No, Sagan," Cassidy was saying.

"Ah, hell," he said, releasing her and stepping back.

"You're angry," Cassidy said with a sad sigh.

He didn't know what he was. Sexually frustrated, that much he knew, but beyond that? Hell, he had emotions churning within him he didn't recognize or welcome; strange, twisting, turning messages he couldn't understand. What was this tiny whisper of a woman doing to him? Yes, he'd settle for anger. That emotion he understood.

"Let's get the hell out of here," he said gruffly. He brushed by Cassidy and strode across the room to the front door. He turned to look at her, where she still stood, in the center of the dance floor. "Come on. I need some sleep. I was suffering from jet lag before I did a stint as a bartender."

"Yes, all right," she said quietly. She crossed the room, retrieved her purse from behind the bar, then joined Sagan at the door. She looked up at him.

"Dammit," he roared, "don't do that!"

She frowned. "Do what?"

"Look at me as though you're scared to death I'm going to throw you on the floor, rip off your zoot suit, and ravish your body. Don't you dare be frightened of me, Cassidy Cole." He flung open the door. "Not ever!"

Cassidy smacked at the light switches and stomped past him.

"Why don't you yell a little, Sagan?" She glared at him before locking the door after them. "Scream in my face. I don't care."

"I'm not yelling," he yelled.

"Oh, shut up and get in the car. Or walk home. Or take a long stroll off a short pier. I don't give diddly-squat what you do."

"Diddly-squat? Nobody says 'diddly-squat.' "

"It's on par with 'ravish your body,' " she said. poking him in the chest with her finger. " 'Ravish your body' indeed. That's so-o-o corny. Do you want a ride or not?"

"I'll drive."

"Not a chance, Jones," she said. She marched to the driver's side of her compact car and opened the door. "The mood you're in, you'd probably wrap us around a telephone pole." She slid behind the wheel and yanked the door closed.

Sagan strode to the passenger side, pulled open the door, and peered in.

"Wonderful," he said. "I can't fold myself into a pretzel, Cassidy. How am I supposed to fit in there?"

"Wing it," she said, smiling sweetly. "Or walk."

Sagan cut loose with a string of expletives that caused Cassidy to roll her eyes heavenward as he edged his massive body into the small car. She started the engine and backed out.

"Easy," Sagan said. "One bump and I'll have a knee in my mouth."

"Tsk, tsk. And it would be a knobby knee, to boot."

Sagan glowered at her.

The crackling tension in the car was nearly palpable as Cassidy drove above the speed limit to cover the half-dozen blocks to her apartment. She made no attempt to avoid the ruts in the road, and simply ignored Sagan's colorful comments at each jarring jolt. She screeched to a halt outside the apartment complex.

"Home, sweet home," she said brightly.

"You," Sagan said, opening the car door, "are a menace on the road. Another block, and I probably would have suffered permanent damage."

"Pshaw," Cassidy said, opening her own door. "Keep your voice down. All my neighbors are asleep."

Inside the living room Cassidy planted her hands on her hips and looked at the sofa.

"Let's see,'" she said. "Sheets, pillow, blanket. Check."

"You really expect me to sleep on that thing? Half of me hangs off of the end."

"My dear man," she said, "you are the one who decided to stay here. I have no intention of giving up my bed for you."

He flashed her a dazzling smile. "We could *share* your bed, you know."

"Not on your life, buster."

"Didn't think so," he muttered.

Cassidy went into the bedroom, returned with an armload of linens, and dumped them onto the sofa.

"There," she said. "Good night."

"I'd like to take a shower."

"Now?"

"Now." He pulled his shirt over his head and dropped it onto the floor.

Oh-h-h, Cassidy moaned silently, not that chest. She couldn't handle seeing that magnificent, scrumptious chest. Not while her body was still humming with the desire that Sagan had stirred within her. That chest was no illusion, nor was the rest of Sagan's nonstop self, including those incredible kissin' lips. She really couldn't deal with this.

"Fine," she said. "Take a shower. I'll have a cup of tea while I'm waiting for the bathroom. Oh, and you're an excellent bartender, Sagan. I didn't have a chance to tell you that. I appreciate your filling in for Barry. Of course, you're only staying for a couple of days, but I was rather vague about that so Barry would think you'll be here the entire time he's in Jasper. He's so worried about Barbie, and—"

"Cassidy."

"You know where the clean towels are, so help yourself, and—"

"Cassidy."

"What?"

"Thank you for the dance."

"Don't you do it," she warned. "Don't you dare use that rumbly, sexy voice on me, Sagan Jones. And don't mention that dance, because the next thing I know you'll be discussing those kisses, and I refuse— Are you listening to me?—refuse to discuss those kisses, or the way you made me feel when you . . . or how wonderful it was when . . . Oh, shut up." She spun around and went into the kitchen.

Sagan chuckled softly and followed slowly behind her. He leaned his shoulder against the doorjamb of the kitchen, and watched as Cassidy ran water into a teakettle and banged it onto the stove. She folded her arms over her breasts, stared at a spot on the wall, and tapped her foot.

"I know you're there," she said stiffly, "but I'm ignoring you. Go take a shower."

"I will, in a minute," he said, closing the distance between them. "Look at me."

"No."

"Look at me." He gripped her chin lightly with his fingertips and turned her face to meet his gaze. "Cassidy, anything I say right now is probably going to sound like a line, a bunch of bull, but it isn't, I swear it. That dance, those kisses, holding you in my arms, was wonderful. You're turning me inside out, Cassidy Cole, and I haven't figured out why. But please don't ever be frightened of me. I'd never hurt you, never take more than you were willing to give. It's very important to me that you believe that."

"I think . . ." Cassidy began, then swallowed nervously. "I think that I'm more frightened of myself, Sagan, and of how you make me feel. *I've* always been the one to decide how much of a relationship I wanted with a man. *I* called the shots. That sounds arrogant, I guess, but that's just the way it was. But with you—I don't know, Sagan, it's different. It's as though you're pushing some invisible buttons of mine, or something." She paused, and frowned. "Lust. That's what it is. This must be the first time I've experienced good old-fashioned lust."

"Hey, now, wait a minute," he demanded. "That's not right. There's more happening between us than just lust."

"Such as?"

"Such as . . ." He ran his hand over the back of his neck. "Hell, I don't know. But it's something."

"Lust," she said, nodding decisively. "Goodness, that makes me feel a lot better. I hate to have things controlling me that I don't understand. Biological urges, physical attraction, those I can certainly understand." She squinted at the ceiling. "So this is lust in its purest form. Fascinating."

"Would you knock it off?"

"Why are you yelling again?"

"I'm not!"

"You most certainly are. Go take your shower."

"Look, I don't deny that I want to make love to you, Cassidy, because I do. And you want me. But I won't let you call what's happening between us 'lust.' No, sir, no way."

"Well, excuse me, Mr. Jones, but I don't know how better to describe it."

"It's . . . Or maybe it's . . ." He raked a restless hand through his hair. "Then again, it could be . . . Dammit, I don't know."

"Lust," Cassidy repeated.

Sagan threw his hands up. "Don't say that again."

"Oh, for Pete's sake, don't get so upset. I can't believe for one minute that you're so sensitive. Don't try to tell me you haven't had your share of being the lustee, or lustor, or whatever the heck it is."

"This is different," he roared.

"Pshaw. You're certainly making a hoopla out of this. Anyway, now that I've discovered why I go leaping into your arms every two seconds, I won't do it anymore. It was all very nice, you understand, and your kisses are real zingers, but I don't care to be a lustee, or a lustor, or whatever I am. Therefore I don't intend ever again to—"

"That's it," Sagan declared, pulling her into his arms. "That's all."

Sagan's mouth came down hard on Cassidy's, and her eyes flew open in shock. He lifted her until her toes just barely balanced on the floor, and she had a fleeting image of herself as a green-and-yellow clown being transformed into a marionette.

But then all conscious thought fled her mind, and there were only sensations; the feel of Sagan's mouth on hers, his tongue meeting hers, his aroma, his taste, his heat. She slid her hands slowly up his steely chest, glorying in the feel of the dark, curly hair beneath her palms. She found his nipples, and felt his muscles tense as her hands continued their journey up to twine around his neck. He gathered her close, and the kiss intensified.

Lust, Cassidy thought dreamily, was delicious, mind-boggling, beyond the scope of her wildest imagination. The combination of lust and Sagan Jones produced desire like nothing she had ever known. Lord, how she wanted him.

Sagan lifted his head a fraction of an inch to draw air into his lungs, then claimed Cassidy's mouth once more and plunged his tongue deep inside. He drank of her sweet taste, her aroma, savored the feel of her soft curves that pressed against his aching arousal.

Lust be damned, his mind raged. This was more. This was need and want that touched his soul as well as his body. This was the filling of an empty chill within him with warmth and an unnamed entity. No, he didn't understand what was happening to him with Cassidy, but he knew, *he knew*, it was more than lust.

"Cassidy," he murmured softly. "Ah, Cassidy."

She slowly opened her eyes. "Sagan?"

"Yes," he said, moving her gently away from him. "Enough. But that, Cassidy Cole, was *not* lust. That was more, much more, and you know it."

"No, I don't," she said breathlessly.

"Mmm."

"If you're going to be so articulate, go take a shower."

"Good idea." He started for the door. "An ice-cold shower." He glanced at her over his shoulder. "By the way, that water will boil a lot quicker if you turn on the heat." He left the kitchen.

Cassidy looked at the teakettle. The last thing she wanted now was a cup of tea. She was still all too aware of the flutter of desire deep in her belly.

She'd done it again, she realized. Sagan had touched her, and she'd melted. He'd kissed her, and she'd gone berserk. Absurd. When she felt lust, she didn't mess around. And it *was* lust, despite Sagan's rantings and ravings to the contrary. Why was he so determined to read more into what was happening between them than was there? Wouldn't a temporary visitor, a drifter, be more inclined to tell it like it was, and then take off? Sagan Jones wasn't making much sense.

Neither was she. Her behavior in regard to one

Mr. Sagan Jones was not even close to the norm. She could lecture herself from here to Sunday, but if Sagan zoomed back into that kitchen, she'd probably fall right into his arms again. Disgusting. Delicious, but disgusting.

"You wanton hussy, you," she said to her reflection in the teakettle. "You ought to be ashamed of yourself."

"Bathroom's free," Sagan called from the living room.

Cassidy left the kitchen, then stopped when she saw Sagan covered with the blanket and stretched out on the floor.

"What are you doing down there?"

"Beats folding up on that sorry excuse for a sofa. Go away. I'm sleeping." He closed his eyes.

"You can't sleep on the floor."

"You have rules posted in this hotel? Shh. I'm sleeping."

"You'll ache all over, Sagan. This is ridiculous."

"I've survived worse. Do you think a guy could get some sleep around here?"

"Oh, of course," she said, turning off the light. "Well, good night."

"Yeah."

Cassidy stood and stared at the large lump on the floor outlined by the moonlight streaming in the window. She started toward the bedroom, then stopped, turning to look at Sagan again.

"Darn it, Sagan," she said, "are you trying to make me feel guilty because I won't give you my bed?"

"Nope. It makes no difference to me that you'd fit on that sofa with no problem. I'm perfectly fine right here on the floor. It's an even exchange for hours of bartending at Illusions. Hard labor for a hard floor. Fair enough." He sighed. "Well, good night, Cassidy. I really am beat. I'll see you in the morning." He paused. "If I can walk."

"Oh, shut up." She turned abruptly, tripped on a plant, and muttered an oath. "You're the most infuriating man I've ever met," she told him as she picked her way around the pots to the bedroom.

"But I'm cute," he called after her.

"You are not!" she shot back. Sexy as all get-out, yes. Cute, no. Cute was cuddly and soft, like bunnies and kittens. Sagan was definitely not cute.

Cassidy took a quick shower, braided her hair into two thick, long pigtails, and donned a pale pink full-length flannel nightgown. She crawled into bed, turned out the light, and pulled the blankets up to her chin.

She heard Sagan groan from the other room.

Don't listen to him, she told herself. She hadn't invited him here, so he could just make do with the sleeping arrangements. Well, the sofa was a bit short for someone of his size, but still . . . No. She was not giving up her bed for Sagan. And she certainly wasn't sharing it with him.

Sagan moaned again. "My old football injury, my old war wound. Oh, Lord."

Cassidy clamped a hand over her mouth as a bubble of laughter threatened to escape from her lips. Sagan deserved an Academy Award for his performance. He was a great moaner and groaner. She wasn't going to budge because of it, but he was putting on quite a show.

She rolled onto her stomach, wriggled into a comfortable position, and closed her eyes. A moment later her eyes popped open, and she strained her ears for more sounds from the actor extraordinaire in the living room.

Silence.

Football injury? Cassidy wondered. War wound? No, don't be silly. He was conning her, playing on her sympathies. He wasn't really in pain. Was he? That floor was probably awfully hard, despite the carpeting, and Sagan was suffering from jet lag, and he'd worked without a break at Illusions, and . . . Oh, dear. She wished he'd start snoring, so she'd know he was sleeping peacefully. But what if he was lying there gritting his teeth in agony against the pain of his football injury and war wound? What if . . . ?

"Oh, rats," Cassidy said, flopping over. She flung back the blankets, then stomped into the living room, nightgown flapping around her ankles. "Sagan!" she yelled.

"What! What! What!" he bellowed, sitting bolt upright. "Cap that fool thing, you idiot. It's going to blow."

"Sagan!"

"Huh? Oh, Cassidy. I thought you were an oil well."

"You were asleep?"

"Yes, of course. Isn't that what I'm supposed to be doing down here on the cold, hard floor?"

"You win," she said, throwing up her hands. "I can't stand it. Take my bed. I'll sleep on the sofa."

Sagan tossed back the blanket and got to his feet. "I wouldn't dream of it. It wouldn't be a gentlemanly thing to do."

"Get . . . in . . . my . . . bed," Cassidy said through clenched teeth, her words measured.

Sagan sighed dramatically. "Yes, but will you still respect me in the morning?"

Sagan's shadowy figure was suddenly outlined in crystal clarity as a cloud passed beyond the moon.

"Oh, good Lord," Cassidy said, clamping a hand over her eyes, "you're nude." And absolutely beautiful. The silvery hue of the moon made him look like a majestic statue. "You're naked in my living room." Her heart had stopped beating. "I can't handle this."

"Madam," Sagan said, pulling her hand away from her eyes, "this happens to be my bedroom at the moment, and I wasn't expecting guests. Besides, you're wearing enough for three people. That nightgown looks like it belongs to someone's grandmother."

"I like it," Cassidy said, peering down at herself. "It's cozy and—How dare you stand there stark naked? March yourself into that bedroom, get in that bed, and cover yourself up this very instant."

Sagan grabbed her by the upper arms, hauled her to him, and planted a loud, wet kiss on her lips.

"You're a peach of a person, kid," he said. "Sleep well." He started across the room.

Cassidy sneaked a tiny peek at his retreating form.

"Nice buns," she said under her breath.

"Thank you," came the reply.

Cassidy blushed crimson and rolled her eyes to the heavens. Laughing softly, she gathered the bed linens from the floor, made up the sofa, and settled in comfortably.

"Good night, Cassidy Cole," Sagan called softly.

"Good night, Sagan Jones.

A few minutes of silence passed, and Cassidy began to drift off to sleep.

"Cassidy?"

"Yes? What?"

"Do I really have knobby knees?"

Cassidy laughed. "Yes."

"No one has ever said a word about my knees before," he said, sounding extremely peeved.

"Well, don't worry about it. If a woman couldn't look past your knees to see the person within you, she isn't worth having. How's that? Feel better?"

He chuckled. "Yes."

"Okay. Good night."

"Right."

Several more minutes of silence passed.

"Cassidy?"

"Who? Oh. Yes?"

"Were you asleep?"

"I guess so. What do you want, Sagan?"

"It isn't just lust."

It was another hour before Cassidy finally slept again.

Four

The ringing of the telephone woke Cassidy early the next morning, and she nearly toppled off the sofa as she reached foggily for the receiver.

"Speak," she mumbled.

"It's Barry. I'm sorry I woke you, but Barbie and I are ready to leave for Jasper. Listen, I talked to Jimmy, and he says he can strip and refinish the dance floor at Illusions now because he's waiting for some parts at his other job. He said he'll hustle with the floor, and it should only take a few days. What do you think?"

"Well, sure, okay," Cassidy said, then yawned. "We agreed it had to be done, and we've put the money aside for it. This is as good a time as any, I suppose."

"I'll call him back and tell him to go ahead. I'll stop by and leave a key for him, then put a sign on the door saying we're temporarily closed. It'll do you good to have some time off, Cassidy. Well, I've got to get going."

"Just concentrate on Barbie. We'll all be thinking of you, Barry."

"Thanks. 'Bye."

Cassidy slowly replaced the receiver, then sank back against the pillows. Time off, she repeated to herself. Like a vacation? That hinted at hours of relaxation, peace, and quiet, with nothing jangling her nerves.

With Sagan Jones under her roof? Oh, ha! The days ahead while Illusions was closed were not going to be relaxing at all.

But they were. Sort of.

Sagan received the news of the temporary closing of Illusions with a shrug, then volunteered to cook breakfast as long as Cassidy promised to take on the chore of dinner. Lunch, he said, would be a joint effort.

The pattern was set. Cassidy was wakened every morning with a steaming cup of coffee poked under her nose. They spent lazy days going for walks in the desert, reading, trekking to the laundromat, and debating everything from environmental-control laws to the attributes of hothouse tomatoes versus a field-grown crop. No topic was too mundane, too trivial, for lively discussion.

Sagan gave the plants a lengthy dissertation on the safety rules of oil drilling, which Cassidy declared was the most boring sermonette she'd ever heard. It was better, Sagan announced, than reading to the foliage all three copies of the six-page newspaper, *The Cherokee Chatter*, that were delivered each morning, and why would anyone want three copies in the first place?

She wasn't quite sure how that had happened,

Cassidy explained, except that the kids selling subscriptions were just so cute and . . . Well, she suddenly had three papers. Sagan had laughed.

Having Sagan around was fun, for the most part pleasant, comfortable, and, to Cassidy's amazement, very, very nice. He would give her a good-night kiss on the forehead, then go into the bedroom, leaving her smiling at the knowledge that he was only a room away.

But there was always an undercurrent of awareness, a hum of sexuality, that never completely dissipated. Cassidy would look up from the book she was reading, to find Sagan's eyes on her. A long, sensuous moment would pass; then they would redirect their attention to the forgotten pages in front of them. An accidental brushing of bodies in the tiny kitchen would cause waves of nearly palpable sexual tension to wash over and through them.

It was with mixed feelings of relief and disappointment that Cassidy approved Jimmy's work on the dance floor, and Illusions reopened on Thursday. It was Cowboy Night, and Cassidy was thrilled when Sagan went so far as to deck himself out in a royal-blue western shirt. He simply rolled his eyes, however, when she appeared again in her clown suit on Friday.

When Cassidy awoke just after noon on Saturday, she was sprawled, as usual, on her stomach on the sofa. She opened one eye, saw nothing more than a large green plant, and shut her eye again.

Sagan! Both her eyes popped open. He must still be asleep, she thought, since he hadn't shoved the usual mug of lifesaving coffee at her, which she so thoroughly enjoyed.

With a groan she rolled onto her back and blinked

against the bright sunlight filling the room. She laughed softly.

It certainly sounded racy, she thought. Sagan Jones was in Cassidy Cole's bed. What kept the whole scenario from qualifying for worldly and sophisticated was that Cassidy Cole had spent all those nights on the sofa. Oh, well. She'd never considered herself worldly and sophisticated in the first place. In spite of living in an affluent section of San Francisco, her parents hadn't hobnobbed with the rich and famous. Cassidy had never been a part of the jet set, and didn't particularly feel that she'd missed anything. She was just Cassidy, nothing fancy or phony.

And Sagan? she mused. Who was Sagan? An oil driller with no family. A man who knew how to tend bar and charm the socks off every woman who crossed his path. A man with kissin' lips, a nonstop body, and eyes that could melt bones.

A man who had said that what was happening between him and her wasn't just lust.

"Oh, pshaw," Cassidy said, swinging her feet to the floor. Of course it was lust, she told herself. What else could it be? What else but lust could cause such new, wondrous, nearly indescribable sensations to swirl within her when Sagan held and kissed her? What, if not lust, caused her heart to do a funny little cartwheel whenever her gaze met his? Yes, it was lust creating the strange ache deep inside her and the flush on her cheeks at the mere image of Sagan in her mind. Lust was potent stuff. "Amazing," she said, getting to her feet.

Cassidy hiked up her nightgown, stepped over several plants, and went to the open bedroom door.

She peered in, then frowned slightly as she saw the neatly made bed. No Sagan. A peek into the kitchen revealed a pot of coffee kept warm in the coffee maker. But no Sagan. Her frown deepened to a scowl as she returned to the bedroom and dressed in jeans and a lightweight blue sweater. She braided her hair into a single plait that hung down her back, then wandered into the kitchen for a cup of coffee.

No, she argued with herself, she wasn't disappointed that Sagan wasn't there; she was just surprised. But the apartment was empty, and very, very quiet.

"He's gone," she said aloud, her eyes widening, "caught the bus to Jasper." Wait a minute, she told herself. Calm down. Even as blurry-eyed as she'd been, she remembered now that she'd seen Sagan's shaving gear in the bathroom, and his duffel bag was on the floor of the bedroom.

She smiled and sank onto a chair at the table. Sagan wasn't gone. He simply wasn't there at the moment. Heavens, she'd felt a rush of—What had that been?—at the thought of his leaving without so much as a "good-bye," a "see you around." Had she felt panic? No, that was absurd. Sadness? Anger? No, none of those. It had been . . . Oh, mercy, it had been . . .

Loneliness.

Cassidy's grip tightened on her coffee mug, and she stiffened in her chair. She let the word *lonely* penetrate her mind, her heart, her soul, then shivered, as though a chill wind had accompanied the word.

It didn't make sense, she thought. She'd never been lonely in her entire life. Her absentee parents had made it necessary for her to learn early on to rely on herself. Beaver had been there, but he'd been older, had things he'd wanted to do without a little sister tagging along. She was comfortable with herself, enjoyed her own company, and through all the years had never been lonely.

Then why, she wondered, had it been loneliness that had assaulted her when she'd thought that Sagan had gone? As foreign as the emotion was to her, she knew that that was what it had been. Why? Why would the departure of a man who had barely touched her life have such a devastating effect on her? If it was because of the lust, then that was sick. Really sick.

No, Cassidy realized, that wasn't what had thrown her for a loop. The idea of Sagan Jones, the man, the person, exiting stage left from her life had caused the chill of loneliness. Sagan filled her little home to overflowing with his vibrant masculinity, his smile, laughter, the rich, rumbly timbre of his voice. He had made her so acutely aware of her own femininity, the part of her that was pure woman. With Sagan gone, there was a glaring void; the counterpart, the other half, called man, was missing.

Cassidy got to her feet, went into the living room, and stared down at a group of plants.

"This will never do," she told them. She wouldn't allow it, she silently vowed. Sagan Jones was not staking a claim on her day-to-day life, her space, or, most importantly, her heart. He was there temporarily, just passing through, and it wouldn't matter one bit when he left. She'd been alone before, and she'd be alone again. Fine. But oh, darn, why did the image of "alone" keep creeping closer to the newly discovered emotion of "lonely"? No, this definitely would never do. "Got that?" she said to an African violet. "It's time to get my act together."

Cassidy busied herself putting away the bed linens from the sofa, then watered the twenty-two plants, having no idea whether they needed a drink or not. To keep her promise to Mrs. Henderson, she chattered nonstop to her potted guests, finally reciting the Declaration of Independence when she couldn't think of anything else to say. And through it all, one thought niggled at her mind: Where was Sagan?

He could have left her a note. That would have been the considerate thing to do. Not that he was accountable to her, but still . . . There weren't exactly a zillion things to do in Cherokee on a Saturday, or on any day, for that matter, so where could he be? Well, it was none of her business, and besides, she really didn't care, as long as he showed up in time to tend bar at Illusions. But where was he?

"Oh, Cassidy, shut up," she said aloud, shaking her head.

"That's not a very nice way to speak to yourself," a deep voice said.

Cassidy spun around. "Sagan," she said, knowing there was a bright smile on her face. Oh, he was beautiful. Dressed in soft, faded jeans and a black T-shirt, he was absolutely scrumptious. "You were shopping?" she asked, glancing at the grocery bag he held in his arms.

"Yep," he said, heading for the kitchen. Cassidy was right behind him. "I went for a walk, just strolling around looking the town over. Then I picked up a few things. You were dead to the world when I left." And she'd looked like an angel while she slept. He'd stood by the sofa and stared at her, losing all track of time. "Had lunch?"

"No," she said, joining him at the kitchen counter.

"Ham, cheese, fresh fruit." He started to unpack the sack. "Potato chips and the biggest package of chocolate-chip cookies they had. I'm crazy about chocolate-chip cookies. Do you know how long it's been since I've had a chocolate-chip cookie? Maybe I'll skip the other stuff, and start right in on them."

Cassidy laughed. She laughed because Sagan was acting like an adorable little boy, all charged up over chocolate-chip cookies. And she laughed because she was happy—inside, outside, head-to-toe happy. The laughter warmed her, filled her, chased away the earlier chill of loneliness that had crept inside her. Sagan was back. And she registered a wonderful sense of joy.

Sagan tore open the package of cookies, then closed his eyes as he inhaled the tantalizing aroma.

"Bliss," he said, lifting out a cookie. "Would you look at this? It's a work of art." He took a bite. "Oh-h-h, that's fabulous." He turned to Cassidy. "Here. Try it. I'm telling you, this is one great cookie."

Cassidy glanced at the cookie that Sagan held in his hand, looked up at his face, then at the cookie again. Why not? she thought. She leaned forward and sank her teeth into the treat, biting off a large piece. Sagan smiled at her, then popped the remaining morsel into his mouth. They were standing close, so close, and black eyes and blue met and held.

There was nothing sensuous, Cassidy told herself, about sharing a chocolate-chip cookie with a man. Her lips following where his had been. Oh, for Pete's sake, it was only a stupid cookie!

"This is nuts," Sagan said, his voice low. "How is it possible that you can turn me inside out over a damn cookie? I hate to think what's going to happen when we get to the heavy-duty stuff, like ham sandwiches. What are you doing to me, Cassidy?"

"Don't know," she said, her voice sounding strange to her own ears.

Sagan cradled her face in his large hands. "Oh, Cassidy, something is happening between us that I don't understand, and I'm not sure I like it. And it's not just lust. There's no running from that. *It's not just lust.* I've got to figure this out. In fact, I've got a helluva lot to figure out, like what I'm going to do with the rest of my life and . . . Ah, damn, don't look at me like that," he said gruffly, then brought his mouth down hard onto hers.

The kiss tasted like chocolate-chip cookies. The kiss was delicious, and so were the sensations that rocketed through Cassidy as she slid her hands up Sagan's chest to clasp them behind his neck. The kiss was urgent, nearly frantic, as he crushed her to him, delving his tongue deep into her mouth as he pressed her tightly against him. He shifted his stance to lean against the counter, spreading his legs slightly to nestle her against him.

And Cassidy went with no question, seeking his heat, his strength, relishing the feel of his arousal pressing hard against her. Her tongue met his, and she answered his demanding mouth with total abandon.

Sagan's hands roved over the slope of her buttocks, pulling her closer, lifting her to meet his throbbing need. Then his fingers inched higher and slid beneath the waistband of her sweater.

A soft sigh of pleasure caught in Cassidy's throat as she felt Sagan's work-roughened hands on the bare skin of her back. Then up, up, nearer to her aching breasts, which yearned for his touch, their soft flesh straining against the wispy material of her bra. His palms cupped the sides of her breasts; then he shifted her away from him just enough to allow his thumbs to stroke the taut buttons of her nipples. Heated desire surged through her body, causing her knees to tremble and her heart to race.

"Oh, Sagan."

His hands moved again to grip the bottom of her sweater and bunch it up beneath her breasts. He looked directly into her eyes as he hesitated, searching for permission to proceed.

Cassidy looked into the night darkness of Sagan's eyes and saw a raw hunger, a level of passion, that caused her breath to catch in her throat again. And she saw more; a flicker of an emotion she couldn't name, though it tore at her heart, pulled at her senses. There was a need within Sagan that went beyond the physical, something unknown that was calling to her, pleading with her to believe in its existence. She didn't know what it was, but somehow sensed it matched the nameless emotion churning within herself.

She moved her arms to allow Sagan to draw her sweater up and away. He dropped it onto the floor, and her bra followed an instant later. With trembling hands he filled his palms with her breasts.

"Dear Lord," he said, his voice husky with passion, "you're beautiful, exquisite. Ah, Cassidy."

She gasped in surprise as he gripped her waist and lifted her to sit on the counter, moving between her legs to seek her breasts with his mouth. She buried her hands in his thick hair as his lips closed over one breast, suckling, stroking, igniting a flame of heated desire deep, so deep, within her. She pressed his head harder against her, seeking more, offering more, closing her eyes to savor each sensation that coursed through her. Sagan gave the other breast the same loving attention, and the flames of passion within Cassidy licked higher, causing her blood to pound in her veins.

Time and place, reality and reason, disappeared into a hazy mist as Cassidy whispered Sagan's name over and over like a litany. He drank of her sweetness like a thirsty man who knew he must have the precious nectar or perish from the lack of it. The rhythm of his mouth matched the pulsing heat deep inside Cassidy, and she whimpered, wanting more, *needing* more.

Sagan's manhood strained against his jeans, aching with a desire like none he had ever known. But with the needs of his body came the needs of his mind and soul. Through the cloud of passion consuming him he knew that to become one with Cassidy Cole, to make love with Cassidy Cole, would mean passing into her care more than just his seed. She held the power—somehow held the power—to reach deep within him and touch a place no one before her had touched. She could strip him bare, make him vulnerable.

And for the first time that he could remember, Sagan Jones was scared to death.

He drew his mouth from Cassidy's breast, and buried his face in the soft flesh, his breathing rough as he strove for control. His shaking hands roamed restlessly over her back, to her waist, her hips, coming to rest at last on her thighs as he eased himself slowly away from the sweet haven of her body.

He lifted his head, and their eyes met.

Neither spoke.

Currents of sexuality shot between them, back and forth, heated, calling, crying out the needs not being spoken in words.

"Oh, Sagan," Cassidy said finally, hardly above a whisper, "I want—"

"Shh. No," he said, placing two fingers against her lips. "Listen to me, Cassidy, please. I know you want me, and I want you more than any woman I've ever met. But I can't make love to you. I can't because it isn't just lust, but I don't know what it is. Until I do know, until I understand, I can't have you."

"I see," she said, blinking back sudden and unexpected tears.

He cradled her face in his hands. "Do you? Do you really?" He searched her face for an answer.

"I . . . Yes. I've told myself over and over that it was only lust between us, but I guess deep inside I knew that wasn't true. Everything is so different with you, Sagan. I've never felt like this before."

He reached to the floor for her bra and sweater and handed them to her before lifting her off the counter and onto her feet.

"I should leave here," he said. "Leave you alone right now. Get on that crummy bus and disappear." He paused. "But I'm not going to do it. I'll find somewhere else to stay if you want me to, but I'm not leaving Cherokee, not yet. Do you want me to leave your home?"

"No." Cassidy clutched her sweater to her breasts. "You're here when you're not here, so you might as well be here. That didn't make sense."

"Yes, it did," he said, managing a small smile. "Look, go get dressed, and I'll make us a sandwich. Okay?"

"Yes," she said, starting toward the door.

"Cassidy?"

"Yes?" She turned slightly to look at him.

"Please don't be sorry about what happened."

"I'm not."

"You're not frightened of me, are you? I told you I couldn't handle that."

"I know you wouldn't hurt me, Sagan."

"Not physically. I'd never hurt you physically, but there's emotional pain, too, Cassidy. I'd never intentionally hurt you emotionally, but there are no guarantees."

"I realize that." She nodded. "I'll go get dressed."

As she left the kitchen, he ran his hand down his face and drew a deep, shuddering breath that seemed to rip at his soul. He was shaken to the core, confused and angry, aching in mind as well as in body.

You're in trouble, Jones, he told himself. Deep, deep trouble. He felt as though he were stumbling around in a dark cave looking for a way out, though he didn't know what he'd find when he got there. Would there be warmth, sunshine, happiness? Or would there be only cold and the greatest misery he'd ever known?

"Ah, hell."

•   •   •

In the bedroom Cassidy quickly redressed, then splashed cold water on her flushed cheeks. She sank onto the edge of the bed, and stared at her hands, which were clenched tightly in her lap.

Well, she thought, then drew a wobbly breath. Just . . . well.

She threw up her hands, then fell backward on the bed, looking up at the ceiling.

She felt as though she'd been sent to her room like a naughty child. There'd been no need to go in there to redress, no sense of modesty to protect. After all, Sagan Jones had been the one to take her things off in the first place. Then he'd sent her away and . . . No, she wasn't being fair, and she knew it. Sagan was giving them both time to calm down. Or, to be more precise, cool off.

Cassidy waited for a wave of guilt over her behavior in the kitchen to assault her, but it never came. Instead, a soft smile formed on her lips as she relived each moment with Sagan. He had been so strong yet so gentle, and the feel of his mouth on her breasts had ignited a flame of passion within her like nothing she had ever known before. Beyond the physical pleasure had come the realization that it was right and good to offer herself to Sagan. She would have become one with him with no hesitation, no regrets.

Oh, yes, this was more than lust.

Her feelings for Sagan, Cassidy knew, were growing, taking her slowly forward to a place where she had never been. She was hovering on the brink, though cautious still, filled with both yearning and trepidation, but teetering close, so close to . . . love.

Love. Being in love. Loving Sagan.

She sifted the words through the chambers of her

mind, her heart, her soul, trying them on for size. Was it true? she wondered. Was she actually falling in love with Sagan? How would she know if this new and tempestuous emotion within her was love? And if she did love for the first time in her life, had she chosen wisely?

The answer came quickly. No, not really. Sagan was passing through, would leave as quickly as he had come. And he could very well take her heart with him when he left. And there she'd sit, Cassidy thought dismally, crying her little eyes out, the newly discovered emotion of loneliness keeping her company, and wondering, once again, how she had gotten herself into such a mess. Darn, this wasn't going well at all.

Cassidy sat up and smoothed her hair. And what about Sagan? she mused. He, too, was experiencing new and strange feelings. His confusion over those emotions had kept him from making love to her. Could it be, was it possible, that Sagan was falling in love with her? Oh, heavens, imagine that.

No, it wouldn't matter, she thought. Sagan was tough, strong, would stay in control of himself. If he discovered that he had indeed fallen in love with her, he'd no doubt be satisfied to know at last what had gotten him into a tailspin. Then he'd disappear into the sunset. His determination to stay in Cherokee for now stemmed from the fact that he was facing an unknown entity within himself, and he didn't like that, not one little bit. Sagan Jones called the shots, ran the show, and at the moment he was mad as hell because invisible forces were pushing and pulling him apart.

Cassidy sighed. She could picture it all so clearly

in her mind. A little light bulb would go on over Sagan's head, and he'd realize that, son of a gun, he'd been falling in love with her. Satisfied to have found the answer to his question, he'd tool off to Tulsa without a backward glance. That rat.

And if her light bulb made her realize the same thing about Sagan? The way her luck ran, the bulb would glow brighter and brighter, get stronger, and she'd have no idea how to turn it off.

How did a person not fall in love with another person, especially if you didn't want to fall in love with that person? she asked herself.

"I'm asking me?" she mumbled. "How in the heck should I know?" It would be really stupid to fall head over heels in love with Sagan, and she knew that. She also knew that if it was going to happen, there wasn't a darn thing she could do about it. "I don't even care that he has knobby knees."

"Cassidy," Sagan called, "come have a sandwich."

"When in doubt, eat," she said, then left the bedroom.

In the kitchen, Sagan waved her to a chair at the table without really looking at her. He had made huge ham-and-cheese sandwiches, poured glasses of soda, and put the potato chips, fruit, and chocolate-chip cookies on the table. He sat down opposite her and began to eat, concentrating on his sandwich as though it were his first introduction to ham and cheese.

Cassidy took a bite and chewed slowly, well aware that Sagan was extremely tense. The knot in her stomach told her that she wasn't in such terrific shape herself. This would never do.

"So," she said, a trifle too loudly, "tell me about

yourself, Sagan." Oh, Lord, what a dumb thing to say. She'd seen the man naked, she'd been half naked herself, and she said casually, "Tell me about yourself," as though he'd just arrived. Oh, boy.

Sagan looked at her with a slight frown on his face. "Tell you about myself? Like what? You know who I am."

"No," Cassidy said thoughtfully, "not really. Now that I think about it, I know very little about you."

He shrugged. "There's not much to tell. I've been an oil driller in foreign countries for our government for the past ten years."

"And now?"

"And now I quit."

"Why?"

"I don't know. I woke up one morning and decided I'd had enough. I was tired of moving around, having no roots, no sense of permanence. So I hauled myself back to the States. First stop, Cherokee, Arizona. All I have to do now is figure out what to do with the rest of my life." He shook his head. "Brother, I don't even have a clue. All I know is that I don't want to see another oil well. I guess I'll steer clear of Texas."

"Good idea," she said, nodding. "Sagan, you said you didn't have any family. What happened to your parents?"

"What are you?" he asked gruffly. "The CIA?"

"I'm sorry." She toyed nervously with her sandwich. "I didn't mean to pry."

Sagan sighed. "You're not prying. I'm just not used to talking about myself. It's not a very interesting story, Cassidy. My mother skipped out when I was ten, and my father was a drunk. I ran away when I was sixteen, and passed myself off as being older. I worked at anything and everything in Chicago, some legal, some not, then finally signed on as an oil driller. They were looking for muscle, and didn't ask a lot of questions. It paid big bucks. I've got a helluva lot of money stashed away, and I can go wherever I choose. That's it. I told you it wasn't very interesting."

Cassidy frowned as she watched Sagan redirect his attention to his lunch. Sagan had told his life story with a blasé attitude, but she'd seen the flicker of pain cross his features and settle into the dark pools of his eyes.

Cassidy pictured in her mind the sad and lonely little boy that Sagan must have been, growing up unloved and neglected. He had played the role of an adult far earlier than he should have been expected to, never knowing the warmth and caring that she and Beaver had experienced. Then Sagan had spent years in foreign countries, again with no home, no knowledge of what a family and love could bring to him. And he was hurt, she knew it, filled with a pain so deep, he might not even be willing to acknowledge its existence to himself.

Her heart ached for him. She wanted to throw her arms around him and comfort the part of him that was harboring the cold and lonely memories of his past. How incredible it was that Sagan had grown to be a man of such gentleness and sensitivity. How easy it would have been for him to lash out at the world in retribution for all that he had been denied.

But not Sagan. Oh, no, Cassidy thought, not her Sagan. He was like no man she had ever known. He touched her soul as well as her body with a gentle hand and a depth of caring. His dark eyes had searched her face for reassurance, acceptance, waiting to know that she wanted what he offered her as their desires soared.

And she did want him. But not, Cassidy realized, just the ecstasy of at last being one with him, feeling his magnificent body mesh with hers, become a part of her, make her complete. No, it was more than that. She wanted Sagan, the man, all of him. She'd hear his laughter, see his smile and match it with her own. The newly discovered chill of loneliness within her would be warmed by Sagan, and she would do the same for him. They were separate entities, each an individual, but together they would be overflowing with joy, sunshine . . .

And love.

Sudden tears filled Cassidy's eyes, but she blinked them away and forced her trembling hands to lift her sandwich to her mouth for a small bite, her gaze still riveted on Sagan. In her mind's eye she saw her silly light bulb, and it was glowing so brightly, it nearly blinded her with its intensity. The doubts were gone, the questions answered, the decision reached by forces out of her control.

She was in love with Sagan Jones.

"Oh, dear," Cassidy said, not realizing she had spoken aloud.

Sagan glanced up at her. "What's wrong?"

"What? Oh, nothing. I was just noticing that this is a big sandwich. I don't think I can eat it all."

"I'll polish off what you can't handle. Are you all right? You look a little pale."

"Oh, yes, I'm fine," she said, forcing a smile. Absolutely dandy, she thought dryly. She was in love for the first time in her life, and she'd chosen a man who was just passing through town. She was as dumb as the farmer's daughter who took up with the traveling salesman.

"Oh, dear," she said again.

Sagan frowned. "Cassidy, what is it? You sound . . . you even look . . . I don't know, sad, or something."

"Sad? Me? Nope, not me. I'm happy as a clam, Miss Sunshine herself. So tell me, Sagan, what did you see during your walk around Cherokee? Anything interesting?"

"It's a nice little town; friendly people, everything is clean, shows pride of ownership. I met the sheriff. Of course he'd already heard all about me. He told me the story of your rooster with the sore toe, and he laughed so hard that his face turned purple."

"Is that so? Well, he sure was a grouch when he showed up here at two A.M. to evict my poor bird. Do you know that the sheriff came in full uniform? I think he sleeps in it. That uniform is his pride and joy."

"He seemed like a nice guy."

"He is . . . most of the time. Anyway, you sort of like Cherokee, huh?" she said. Oh, Cassidy, stop it, she scolded herself. She was grabbing at straws, pretending that Sagan was about to launch into a glowing report on Cherokee, Arizona, that would sound like a prerecorded message from the Chamber of Commerce. Sagan Jones was *not* about to announce that Cherokee was what he'd always been looking for in the way of a permanent home, that Cassidy was the love of his life, and why didn't they quit messing around, get married, and raise a slew of little Joneses? No, Sagan wasn't going to say any of those things. The rotten bum.

"Yeah," Sagan said, "it's a nice town. Quiet, but nice. Don't you miss the social scene of San Francisco, though?"

"No."

"The theater? Shops? Parties?"

"No."

"Oh," he said with a shrug. "I can see why Illusions is such a success. It's the only bar in town."

"Club, not bar."

"Whatever. You could expand your services, you know. Offer sandwiches and desserts, and open a little earlier."

"Well, it would take a lot of organizing, and would mean hiring extra people. Barry wouldn't want to take on longer hours because of Barbie and the baby. There aren't that many people on the loose here looking for work."

"It was just a thought. Illusions has a lot of potential. It's a sharp place, Cassidy. You should be very proud of yourself. I intend to tell Beaver that you're doing just great here."

Oh, ha! Cassidy thought. Falling in love with the wrong man was not great. Heading down a road toward guaranteed heartbreak was not great. A lot Sagan Jones knew. She wasn't doing great at all.

"Thank you, " she said, then took a bite of sandwich.

"So what's on your agenda for this afternoon?" he asked.

"Nothing. I've already watered Mrs. Henderson's twenty-two plants. Why?"

"Well, the sheriff . . . Harry. He insists that I call him Harry."

Cassidy laughed. "Do tell."

"Yep. Anyway, he's got an old Jeep that he said I could use whenever I wanted to. I thought you and I might go for a drive, take a look at the area outside of town. Interested?"

"Very," Cassidy said, smiling.

"Okay. We'll finish up here, then walk over and get the Jeep. Harry said he'd leave the keys in it."

"Harry," Cassidy repeated.

"Yes, we're buddies. Harry is a good man."

"He's totally unsympathetic when it comes to roosters with sore toes."

"Nobody's perfect," Sagan said with a grin. He popped a chocolate-chip cookie into his mouth. "Cookie?"

"No, thanks." Heavens, no, she didn't want a chocolate-chip cookie. That little treat had gotten her into enough trouble for one day. And if she were really smart, she'd tell Sagan to move out of her apartment, and she wouldn't go for a drive with him, and . . . Oh, forget it. She didn't want to be smart when it came to Sagan. She wanted to be with him, share every moment she had left with him, before he took the rickety bus out of Cherokee and out of her life. She'd cherish every one of those moments, tuck them away in a special, private chamber of her heart.

That would be all she had, just memories.

Memories of Sagan Jones.

Five

April in Cherokee, Arizona.

The sky was a clear blue umbrella dotted by an occasional fluffy white cloud that reminded Cassidy of a dollop of whipped cream about to be plopped on top of a mug of hot chocolate. The weather was perfect—warm in the sunshine, cool in the shadows. The aroma of seemingly endless acres of desert wildflowers wafted through the air. Perfect.

Sheriff Harry's Jeep, however, was not perfect, nor was the maniac behind the wheel, Cassidy decided. She was too young to die! "Sagan," she shrieked, clutching the dashboard. "Would you slow down?"

"Can't," he yelled over the noise of the rattling vehicle and the rushing wind. "Have to have momentum to get up this hill."

"Forget the stupid hill."

"Hang on," he hollered, and gunned the engine.

"Oh, Lord!"

Cassidy closed her eyes as the open-top Jeep raced

up the flower-covered hill, sounding as though vitally important parts of the engine were falling out as it went. She tightened her grip on the dashboard until her knuckles turned white, and sent a mental message to Beaver confessing that it had indeed been she who had put glue on the seat of his car when he'd had the date in high school with Clara Sue Rosenthal. If Cassidy Cole was to die, it would be with a clear conscience.

"All right!" Sagan said triumphantly, then turned off the ignition. "What a ride. What a great ride. That was really . . . Cassidy?" He jiggled her arm. "Are you in there?"

She opened one eye, then slowly opened the other. "Oh, Lord, we made it."

"You doubted my ability to drive this thing? I'm crushed. Let's walk around."

"Can't."

"Why not?"

"My fingers won't move."

Sagan chuckled, then pried her fingers loose from the dashboard. He slid his hand to the nape of her neck, and planted a fast, hard kiss on her lips.

"There," he said, smiling. "All better."

"Mmm." She glared at him.

"Come on. I want to look around."

To her own amazement, Cassidy's legs supported her when she slid off of the seat of the Jeep, and she didn't object when Sagan took her hand and led her through the flowers to climb a slope beyond. At the top he stood perfectly still, seeming hardly to breathe.

"What an incredible view," he said in awe. "Nature doing its best as far as the eye can see. Flowers, pecan orchards, mountains. That mountain range is something. It's as though it's standing guard over Cherokee, keeping the rest of the world at bay. This is beautiful country, Cassidy."

"There's peace here, Sagan," she said softly. "And it's not an illusion, it's real. Real peace."

He nodded. "Yes, I can feel it. I'm beginning to understand why you like it here so much. You know, a man would have to be comfortable within himself, with who he was, to live here. There are no phony trappings. There's no fast-paced social scene to hide in. This is straightforward and honest. A lot of people couldn't handle this."

Could Sagan? she wondered. Was he imagining himself settled here, being a part of all that the place offered? Or was he one step back and apart, merely observing for a while before he disappeared over the mountains?

Sagan tugged on her hand and they strolled farther, the bright flowers bending under their feet as sunshine poured over them. Neither broke the comfortable silence by speaking. At the top of another incline, Sagan stopped.

"Let's sit," he said. "I offer you a throne of wild flowers, madam."

Cassidy laughed, and sank to the ground next to him. She picked several flowers and idly began to pull the petals off, watching them float lazily to the grass. A tranquility crept over her, a sense of all things being right, in their proper order and place. Sagan shifted closer to her, and she turned her head to look at him questioningly as she felt a slight pull on her braid.

"I'm putting flowers in your hair," he said quietly. "You'll look like a princess. You'll be the princess of this hill and all the land below."

"Do I have subjects to rule?" she asked, smiling.

"Just the animals. Birds, squirrels, deer. They all come to see you."

She laughed. "And my rooster? What about my rooster?"

Sagan chuckled. "He'll be along as soon as his toe feels better. This is a pretty tough trip for a guy with a sore toe, you know."

" 'Tis true. And since I'm such an understanding princess, I'll wait until he's fit to make the journey. Then I'll gather all my subjects around me and . . ." Cassidy's voice trailed off.

"And?"

She pulled her knees up and wrapped her arms around them as she tilted her face back to receive the warming rays of the sun. There was a whimsical tone in her voice when she spoke.

"I'll gather them close," she continued, "then speak of the peace and beauty of our land, and of how very fortunate we are to live here. Then I'll issue a decree saying there can be only love here; no harsh words, no dissension, only love for one another. From that harmony, the other kind of love will grow. The heart, mind, body, and soul kind of love. Love of commitment, and forever and ever. They'll walk away in pairs, like on the ark, two by two. Then later, there will be babies born of that love—bunnies, squirrels, fawns. Think of it, Sagan. It will never end. The babies will grow up, love, have babies of their own. And they'll tell the legend of the princess on the hill. And . . . oh, my, I'm getting carried away."

"That's a beautiful story," he said, his voice low.

"I could actually see them, the animals. But"—she sighed—"it was just an illusion. Oh, sometimes I wish that illusions were real, that I could create them in my mind, then hold on so tightly, they couldn't disappear."

"What I'm seeing now is no illusion," Sagan said, his voice oddly husky. "I've dreamed of this moment, Cassidy."

"What are you talking about?" she said, turning to look at him.

"Your hair."

"My . . . You undid my braid. I was so wrapped up in my princess illusion that I didn't even realize you were doing it."

Sagan filled his hands with the waist-length hair, then watched it sift through his fingers.

"I knew it would be like this," he said. "Spun gold, silken spun gold. You have the most beautiful hair I've ever seen." He moved to face her, pulling the tresses gently forward to fall over her breasts. "Lord."

Sagan lifted his eyes to meet Cassidy's gaze, and her heart thundered, causing a roaring noise in her ears. In the dark, dark pools of Sagan's eyes she saw raw desire. It went further than the physical, seeming to echo the message of his soul, stripping him bare before her. He was vulnerable, placing himself at her mercy to accept or reject all that he was.

Cassidy's heart nearly burst with love for Sagan.

She lifted her hands, her fingertips lightly tracing his features one by one, etching them indelibly in her mind. And in her heart. A soft smile formed on her lips as she outlined his mouth, hearing his sharp intake of breath.

Then she leaned forward and pressed her lips to his.

Sagan groaned deep in his chest as he opened to

her to receive her questing tongue. He wove his fingers through her thick golden hair, cupping her head with his hands as the kiss intensified. Not breaking the searing kiss, he shifted his weight and hers, laying her back onto the bed of flowers, then following her down onto the fragrant cushion. He rested on his forearms, one leg pinning both of hers in place as their tongues dueled in matching rhythms.

Heat. And need. And a desire swirled within Cassidy that was so deep, so intense, it was near pain, causing her heart to race and Sagan's name to echo in her mind. She slid her hands to his back; roaming hands, hands memorizing every taut, steely muscle beneath her palms. He came closer, his chest crushing her breasts, making them ache for more. Her blood hummed in her veins, tingling, her body crying out for the fulfillment that only Sagan could give her. The needs of her flesh mingled with that of her soul—the need to be loved by Sagan Jones. A soft sob caught in her throat.

Sagan slid his hand down to the waistband of Cassidy's sweater, then beneath it, pressing hard on her soft skin. His manhood surged hard against his jeans, demanding the release that only the sweet haven of Cassidy's body could give him. Voices of confusion warred in his mind, screaming for his attention. He felt as though he were tumbling through a dark tunnel, grasping for reality, then feeling it slip through his fingers.

He wanted, he needed, he had to have, Cassidy Cole.

This was dangerous, like sailing an uncharted course with no map, no sense of direction, no understanding of where he was going. He had to stop. He had to!

Sagan tore his lips from Cassidy's and drew a ragged breath, but in the next instant she lifted her hips to press against him, and a moan escaped his throat as he claimed her mouth again.

A lifetime, he thought hazily. He'd waited a lifetime to make love to Cassidy, to become one with her.

But it would be more, he knew. Cassidy had the power to touch him deep within, to hold fast to the unknown, unnamed emotions churning within him, to stake a claim on his soul, on all that he was. *He* controlled his life, his destiny. He kept himself separate and apart from his emotions, allowing no man, no woman, to step too close or to cross over his carefully drawn, invisible protective line.

Dear heaven, his mind thundered, what would happen to him if he became one with Cassidy? His aching body would find the release it desperately needed, but what of himself? His heart? His mind? His soul? What would she take from him? What would he have passed into her care?

Dammit, he didn't know!

"Sagan," Cassidy whispered, close to his lips. "Love me, Sagan. I want you so much."

No! his mind roared.

But a stronger voice within him reigned supreme. A voice that spoke from the center of the confusion, the emotions that had no name. A voice that silenced his mind, and gathered strength from the heated passion racing throughout him. A voice that uttered one word said in a tone gritty with desire and hardly recognizable as his own.

"Yes."

Oh, thank God, Cassidy thought wildly. She was

to have her Sagan. Here, in their private place, in a bed of nature's gifts, she was to become one with the only man she had ever loved. It was right and good. One. They would be one. Cassidy Cole and Sagan Jones united. Oh, thank God.

Sagan's hand moved upward to just beneath her breasts, then hesitated.

"Cassidy, I—"

"No words, Sagan, please. Love me. I won't be sorry, I promise you. I know what I'm doing." Another sob caught in her throat. "I want you, Sagan. I truly do. Please."

He was lost. The trembling of Cassidy's voice, the tears shimmering in her blue eyes, which mirrored her desire, were his final undoing. With shaking hands he drew her sweater up and away, then removed her bra. His heated gaze traveled over her ivory breasts, his eyes alone causing the nipples to grow taut, the tight buds inviting his mouth to suckle their sweet nectar. He lifted one hand to sift her golden hair through his fingers, and watched as it fell in a soft waterfall over the breasts he yearned to touch and taste.

"Beautiful," he said, his voice raspy. "Just so damn beautiful."

He brushed the silken strands away, then lowered his head to draw one nipple deep into his mouth. His hand slid to the snap on Cassidy's jeans, then inched the zipper down, his fingertips tracing the edge of her bikini panties. His mouth sought her other breast as his fingers moved beneath the lacy material of her panties. Lower. On to the curly nest covering her womanhood. Lower. To her heat, moist, ready, telling him of her desire for him.

"Sagan." Cassidy gasped. "Oh, please. Oh, Sagan."

He lifted his head from her breast, then sought her mouth in a hard, feverish kiss, his tongue plummeting deep into the inner darkness. His fingers moved with the same rhythm as his tongue, bringing a moan from Cassidy's throat. She arched against him, seeking more, wanting more, wanting Sagan.

He drew his mouth from hers to gaze at her face. To reassure himself he called upon his last ounce of control. This had to be what she wanted. He had to be sure that she was coming to him of her own choosing, that he had not manipulated her, as he had so many women before. This was Cassidy, and their joining had to be real, honest, mutually agreed upon. No illusions. Only truth.

Sagan's eyes asked the question.

Cassidy's gave the answer.

A warmth spread through him. A warmth different from the heat of his raging desire.

A warmth of peace, of acceptance, of knowing he was wanted—all of him, not just his body, but himself, the man, as well. The voice in his mind began to whisper its warnings of danger once again, but Sagan refused to listen, refused to heed what he had no wish at that moment to hear. He filled his senses with the sight, the sound, the feel and taste of Cassidy, and the voice was stilled.

"Sagan?"

"Oh, yes. Yes, Cassidy. It will be good, I swear it."

"Oh, Sagan, I know."

He kissed her deeply, then shifted up to draw her jeans and panties down her slender legs, skimming off her shoes in the process. She lay naked before him on the bed of flowers, her hair spread in a golden halo around her. Sagan's heart thundered in his chest.

"You," he said, his voice thick, "are the most exquisite woman I have ever seen."

He pushed himself to his feet and shed his clothes, his gaze riveted on Cassidy's face; watching, waiting for any sign, any flicker of fear as she saw all that he was, all he would bring to the honeyed heat of her femininity. He forced himself to stand statue-still above her as her gaze traveled slowly over him. Never had he felt so vulnerable, so bare, not just in body, but in soul as well. His hands curled into tight fists at his sides, and he clenched his jaw as he waited.

And then Cassidy smiled.

It was a gentle smile, a womanly smile. Slowly she lifted her arms to welcome him back into her embrace. He drew a deep breath, only then realizing he'd hardly been breathing. He stretched out next to her, resting on one arm as he splayed his hand on her flat stomach. Then, for a seemingly endless moment, he gazed into the blue pools of her eyes.

Cassidy's heart nearly burst with love as she looked at him. She knew, just somehow knew, with womanly instincts born with this love for him, what it had cost him to stand above her waiting for her acceptance of all that he was. The body he offered her was magnificent, powerful, beautiful as a sculpted statue bronzed to perfection as the sunlight poured over him. The soul he let her glimpse was battered, wary, not totally trusting. Yet there he had stood, baring to her all that he was, inside and out.

Dear Lord, how she loved this man.

"Love me, Sagan," she whispered.

No more words were spoken. None were necessary. Lips, tongues, and hands said all that and more than words could have conveyed. It was give and take in total abandon, holding nothing back, surrendering completely and glorying in surrender. It was passions rising to a fever pitch as bodies glistened and breathing became labored. It was need. Want. Heat. The sweet pain of waiting, waiting, waiting, until . . .

"Oh, Sagan, please! Please!"

"Yes!"

He filled her. With a thrust that stole the breath from her body, Sagan filled her, slipping his arm beneath her hips to bring her closer yet. Then the rhythm began, slowly at first, then increasing in tempo, beautifully matched, synchronized to perfection. The world faded away into oblivion; the flowers, the sun, the sky overhead disappeared. There was only Cassidy and Sagan, as one, moving higher to a place created only for them. Seeking the summit. Thundering in a pounding rhythm of ecstasy.

"Sagan!"

He felt her tighten around him, felt the spasms sweep through her, saw her eyes drift closed as she whispered his name over and over. He drove once more deep within her to give way to his own release, and joined her in the place where she had gone. He collapsed against her, his strength spent, passed from him unto her, and buried his face in the fragrant cloud of her hair.

Slowly, so slowly, they drifted back. Back to the flowers, the sun, the distant hum of buzzing bees. Back to reality.

Sagan began to shift his weight from Cassidy, only to feel her increase the pressure of her hold around his back. He lifted his head and brushed a fleeting kiss over her lips.

"Are you all right?" he asked. "I was rough with you, Cassidy. I didn't hurt you, did I?"

"Oh, no, Sagan, not at all. It was so wonderful. I have never felt so . . . I flew away, went to a place I didn't know existed, and you were there with me. It's never been like that for me."

"I'm glad. It was very special, very different for me, too, Cassidy. I can't explain it, because I don't understand it myself, but believe me when I say it was special. Okay?"

"Okay," she said, smiling.

"I've got to move before I smash you flat, but you feel so damn good."

"Don't go. I can feel you inside me. You're so strong, Sagan, yet so very gentle. That's a beautiful combination. Oh, Sagan, when you came to me, I nearly burst with joy. I felt so complete, whole. I still do."

He chuckled softly. "I'm moving off you right now, Cassidy."

"Mmm," she said, sliding her hands over his taut buttocks and lifting her hips. "Are you?"

"Yes," he answered, his voice sounding slightly strangled, "I am."

"You're sure?" She slipped one hand between them—low, so very low.

"Positive. I . . . oh, Lord. You're asking for trouble, Cassidy Cole."

"No," she whispered. "I'm asking for you, Sagan Jones. Love me again. Take me to that place again. Come with me, Sagan. Please?"

"Ah, Cassidy," he said with a groan, then brought his mouth down hard onto hers.

And they soared.

They were lifted away once more from all that was real: the flowers, the sunshine, the sounds of nature. Yet the place they traveled to was not an illusion. It was theirs alone, Cassidy's and Sagan's, created for them, belonging only to them. One could not go without the other, and they clung to each other, calling aloud the name of the one each held so tightly as they burst upon the place of ecstasy.

"Sagan."

"Ah, Cassidy."

They lingered, then returned, reluctantly, not speaking, just savoring all they had shared. Sagan shifted away, then tucked Cassidy close to his side, sifting the golden silken strands of her hair through his fingers. He gazed down at her flushed face, where she lay nestled against his shoulder, her eyes closed.

Incredible, he thought. Their lovemaking had been like nothing he had ever experienced before. He had given totally of himself, just as he had feared. When he had become one with this exquisite creature, more than their bodies had meshed. His mind, heart, soul had tumbled into a maze that had passed into Cassidy's care along with the physical release of his body.

Dear Lord, no! his mind raged. He didn't want this. He was alone, always had been. He understood it, accepted it, knew it for what it was. He controlled his own life. The restlessness, the emptiness, the loneliness he'd felt when he'd returned to the States was temporary. It had to be. He'd push aside the strange new emotions churning within him because of Cassidy and move on. Leave Cherokee. Leave Cassidy.

He would not, *could not*, give Cassidy Cole his life, his soul, the very essence of himself. He would not give her the power to shatter him, destroy him, bring him to his knees. He was Sagan Jones, and he stood alone.

Alone, his mind taunted. Always alone. So damn alone..

The way it should be. Alone. He would leave Cassidy before . . . before she could say . . . she didn't want him anymore. Like his mother, his father . . . she wouldn't want him anymore.

"Oh, God," Sagan said, with a moan.

"Sagan?" Cassidy opened her eyes to look up at him. "Sagan, you're crushing me."

"What? Oh." He loosened his hold on her. "I'm sorry. Did I hurt you?"

"No, but what's wrong?"

"Nothing."

"Yes, there is. You've become tense. I can feel it. Sagan, please, tell me."

He slid his arms from around her and sat up, reaching for his clothes.

"I said there's nothing wrong," he said gruffly.

"Are you sorry? Are you sorry we made love?"

Sagan's head snapped around to look at her, a deep frown on his face.

"No," he said. Yes! No? Dammit, he didn't know. "Get dressed, Cassidy. It's getting chilly up here." He got to his feet and pulled on his clothes. "Come on."

Dear heaven, Cassidy thought, what had happened? What was wrong with Sagan? It was as though a dark cloud had settled over him. The chill Sagan spoke of wasn't just from the cooling air, but was emanating from him as well. She could almost feel the wall he was erecting between them, as if it were a tangible thing; solid, unmovable, not an illusion, but frighteningly real. Oh, Sagan, why? Why was he doing this?

Tears misted Cassidy's eyes and her hands trembled as she reached for her clothes. The lovemaking she and Sagan had shared had been so very beautiful, she reaffirmed in her mind. Granted, her sexual experience was limited, to say the least, but not even in her fantasies and daydreams had she imagined that being one with the man she loved would be so glorious. And Sagan had felt it, too, how special it had been. She knew he had. She'd seen it on his face, in his eyes.

And now? she questioned. What was he thinking? Where were his thoughts taking him? Why was he turning his back on her now?

With a sad sigh Cassidy dressed, then dragged her fingers through her hair in an attempt to untangle it. She pulled it over one shoulder and began to braid it.

"No," Sagan said sharply.

"What?" she asked, looking up at him quickly.

"Don't braid your hair. Leave it loose, the way I like it."

Dammit, Cassidy thought in an unexpected burst of anger. "Dammit," she said aloud. "And damn you, Sagan Jones."

"Huh?" he said, surprise evident on his face.

"How dare you?" she said, planting her hands on her hips. "How dare you make love to me, the most beautiful, fantastic love that ever took place between two people in the whole wide world, then switch moods so fast, you make my head spin? That's a rotten thing to do, and I don't appreciate it one bit."

"I—"

"Shut up. What are you, Sagan? An illusion? A wonderful, sweet, gentle man only when you're making love? Then you turn into a crabby rat?"

"Crabby rat?" he repeated, his eyes widening.

"I've heard of moody men, but this is ridiculous. You have a lot of nerve ruining this, spoiling what we shared. I won't stand for this. It's—it's unacceptable." She paused to catch her breath. "So just knock it off! And don't speak to me," she added as a tear slid down her cheek. "Don't speak to me, or touch me, or"—a sob caught in her throat—"kiss me, or anything. Go away, Sagan. Leave me alone." No! Dear heaven, she hadn't meant to say that. She was so hurt and confused by Sagan's behavior, but she didn't want him to go. Not yet, Sagan, please. "I . . . oh, hell," she said, and burst into tears.

"Ah, hell," Sagan echoed. He closed the distance between them and pulled her roughly into his arms. "Oh, Cassidy. Dammit, I never meant to make you cry. Don't cry, okay?"

"Too late," she mumbled into his shirt. She sniffled. "I'm crying."

"I realize that," he said, gently stroking her hair, "but try to stop. Can you do that?"

"No," she said sullenly. "I, for one, cannot"—she hiccupped—"turn my moods on and off like a faucet, the way some people I know can. I feel like crying, and therefore I'm crying."

"Oh." He nodded. "Well, I'll hold you until you're finished. How long do you figure you'll need?"

"Oh, for Pete's sake," she said, wiggling out of his

arms. She brushed the tears off her cheeks. "I don't know how long I'll cry. I'm a woman, not a three-minute egg. Forget it." She stomped around him, and started toward the Jeep.

In two long strides Sagan was next to her. He grabbed her arm and spun her around to face him.

His face, Cassidy thought wildly, looked like a storm about to happen. An angry, tempestuous storm. *He* was angry? *He* was upset? What nerve. *She* was the injured party.

"Get your big paw off my arm, Sagan," she said, narrowing her eyes.

"No."

No? Great. Now what was she going to do? "I'm warning you, Sagan." Oh, wonderful. What did she plan to do? Take him out with one punch? What she'd better do was keep her mouth shut.

"I'm not letting you go until you listen to me, Cassidy. I've been called a lot worse than a crabby rat in my day, but coming from you, it makes me sound like the scum of the earth. Dammit, Cassidy, I told you that what we shared was special, and I meant it. I didn't lie to you. It's the fact that it *was* so special that has me tied up in knots. I've never felt this way before, and I don't like it. This thing . . . this whatever it is that's happening between us is scrambling my brain. I'm not leaving Cherokee until I have myself back on track."

"Oh," she said, smiling. "I see. Well, that's fine." He cared for her. Glory be, he really did. "I understand. Whatever you say, Sagan, is okay."

He squinted at her. "*Now* what are you up to? I thought you were crying."

"I was. I did. But now I'm not. I'm so glad you meant it when you said our lovemaking was special."

"It was," he said softly. "More than you even know. I gave you . . . Never mind. I'm sorry I made you cry. I did switch moods on you pretty quickly there, and it wasn't fair. I have a lot on my mind right now. I'll remember today, this hill, the flowers, making love to the princess of this land. I'll remember it, and cherish it."

'Oh-h-h, how sweet," Cassidy said, her bottom lip quivering.

"No more tears," he said, cradling her face in his hands. "They really upset me." He lowered his head slowly toward hers. "Don't cry for me, ever. I'm not worth it."

"Not worth it? Sagan, I—"

"Shh," he said. "I'm kissing you."

—love you, Cassidy's mind finished. Then she gave way to the sensation of Sagan's mouth on hers.

The kiss was soft and gentle and, oh, so sensuous that Cassidy's knees began to tremble. Sagan's tongue skimmed along her bottom lip, and she met it with her own in a lazy dance before he delved deep into her mouth with his. He dropped his arms around her and gathered her close to his hard body. The kiss was enough to bring fresh tears to her eyes, but she blinked them away, deciding she'd used up her quota for one day.

The kiss was Sagan.

And she loved him.

"Enough," he said, lifting his head, his breathing rough. "It's getting late, and we have to get to the bar."

"Club," Cassidy said breathlessly.

"Whatever." He stepped back and stared up at the sky as he drew a deep, steadying breath. "Illusions."

"What?"

He ran his hand over the back of his neck and looked at her again, a frown knitting his dark brows together.

"It's just weird, that's all. I don't know how to explain it but . . . Cassidy, my entire life I've dealt in reality—cold, hard facts. I didn't always like the way things were, but at least I knew exactly where I stood. But now . . ." He shook his head.

"Now?"

"I came here," he said with a sweep of his arm, "and everything changed. I've been off kilter since meeting you, since arriving in Cherokee. It's as though none of this is real."

"I'm real, Sagan," she said softly. And so was her love for him. But she couldn't tell him that she loved him. Not yet. She knew, she just knew, it wasn't what he wanted to hear. He was waging inner battles against everything he was feeling for her. How did she fight for him? How could she win?

"Even the name of your bar . . . club," Sagan went on, "seems to be sending a message to me. Illusions. Maybe I'm drunk, and I'll wake up and find I'm still overseas, drilling oil."

Cassidy laughed. "Nope. You're in Cherokee, Arizona, you lucky devil, you."

Sagan smiled and trailed his thumb over her cheek. "Yes, I'm in Cherokee, Arizona. I just made love to the most beautiful, most desirable woman I've ever known. That much I know. Beyond that?" He circled her shoulders with his arm. "I'm totally losing it. Come on. Let's go." They started for the Jeep.

"I should have thought to ask Barry for his costumes before he left for Jasper," Cassidy said. "You're bigger than he is, but they probably would have fit you."

"Lady," Sagan said with a snort of disgust, "if you think I'm dressing up like some flaky clown, you're dead wrong. You'll have to take me just the way I am."

With pleasure, Cassidy thought. She'd take Sagan Jones just the way he was with a smile on her lips and love in her heart. Forever.

When they reached the Jeep, Cassidy turned to look at the majestic mountain range. It kept the world out, she mused, but could it keep Sagan in, here, in Cherokee with her? No, nothing and no one could hold Sagan where he didn't want to be.

"Ready?" Sagan said.

"Yes. Let's . . . go home, Sagan," she said, looking directly into his eyes.

He met her gaze for a long moment, then, without speaking, slid behind the wheel and turned the key in the ignition.

Home? he thought dryly. A home for Sagan Jones? Now, *that* was definitely an illusion.

Six

To Cassidy's dismay, the ride down the hill in Sheriff Harry's Jeep was even more harrowing than the ride up. She clutched the dashboard again, closed her eyes, and prayed. At the bottom she shot Sagan a stormy glare. He shrugged with an expression of pure innocence on his face, then started toward town at a more reasonable speed. He pulled into the only gas station and turned off the ignition.

"Howdy, Sagan," the elderly owner said. "Howdy, Cassidy."

"Howdy, Norm," Sagan said. "Top the tank, will ya?"

"You bet," Norm said. "See you been out and around in Harry's Jeep. He must think highly of you, Sagan. This-here Jeep is Harry's pride and joy."

"It's a fine vehicle," Sagan said. "Wouldn't mind owning one like it myself."

"Yuck," Cassidy said under her breath. Sagan chuckled.

"I'll get you that gas," Norm said.

"Thanks, Norm," Sagan said.

Norm? Cassidy thought. She'd always called him Mr. Vincent, in deference to his age. And she called the sheriff, "Sheriff." But Sagan? Oh, not ole charm-the-socks-off-'em Jones. It was Norm and Harry. And now that she thought about it, she'd never seen anyone except the sheriff—Harry—driving this rattling piece of junk. And she suddenly realized that she was pouting again over Sagan's instantaneous acceptance into Cherokee's fold.

She knew why it bothered her, she admitted with a sigh. It was because Sagan *was* accepted, fit in, looked right, in the town hidden behind the mountains that shielded it from the world. The people knew Sagan could easily become one of them.

Everyone except Sagan knew that he had found his home. And Cassidy knew that in Cherokee, Arizona, Sagan was loved.

But he would leave, she thought dismally. Just as soon as he'd squared away his feelings for her, found a mental slot to stuff her into so he could forget her, he'd go. The bozo. Why didn't he stop fighting with himself, love her to pieces, and grow old with her in Cherokee?

"See ya, Norm," Sagan said, bringing Cassidy from her reverie.

"Take care, now, Sagan," Norm said. "Take care, now, Cassidy."

" 'Bye, Mr. . . . Norm," Cassidy said, waving. "Oh," she gasped as the Jeep shot forward.

Sagan drove a block farther and parked the Jeep in the spot where he'd picked it up. Cassidy slid off the seat, and they started toward her apartment.

Neither spoke, and it wasn't a comfortable silence. Sagan was tense again, Cassidy realized, stealing a glance at him from beneath her lashes. He appeared casual and relaxed, with his thumbs hooked in the front pockets of his jeans, but he wasn't, and she knew it. He was like a taut wire being wound tighter and tighter.

Inside her apartment, Cassidy forced a lightness into her voice. "My turn to cook," she said, smiling at Sagan. "Would you like an omelet?"

"That's fine. I'll shower now, while you're fixing dinner."

"Okay," she said, watching him make his way around the plants to get to the bedroom. The bedroom, she mused. Was it now *their* bedroom, after what they had shared in the field of wild flowers? Would Sagan automatically assume that they would be sleeping together during the remainder of his stay in Cherokee? Such audacity. Oh, who was she kidding? Of course it was their bedroom.

With a frown on her face and a heavy step, Cassidy went into the kitchen. A few minutes later the aroma of freshly brewed coffee wafted through the air, along with the tantalizing scent of onions and peppers frying.

"Smells good," Sagan said from the doorway.

Cassidy glanced at him, then redirected her attention to the mixture in the pan. "This is going to be a superb omelet, sir," she said. Black cords, pale yellow dress shirt open at the neck, hair damp, thick, begging her fingers to sink into its ebony depth. Couldn't Sagan, just once, look blah, ordinary, nothing to shout about, nothing to send her body into overdrive? No, she guessed not. "Sit down, Sagan. This will be ready in a jiffy."

Sagan sat in a chair next to the table, then rocked back on two legs of the chair, lacing his hands behind his head. Hands, he admitted, that were aching to stroke the golden cascade of Cassidy's hair, then move forward to cup her breasts, which fit his palms to perfection. Hands that now knew her body as well as he knew his own. Lord, she was beautiful. And passionate. And warm, honest, real. She was just so damn fantastic, so . . . everything a woman should be. The incredible, really incredible part, was that now, in this moment, she was his. His! Sagan Jones's woman, his lady, his lover.

Only for now, his mind taunted. This was all temporary. He was passing through Cherokee on his way to . . . where? Hell, he didn't know.

What if . . . He thudded the chair back onto all four legs. What if he stayed? Oh, sure, he thought with a shake of his head. Hang around like an idiot to take it in the chops, to hear Cassidy tell him it had been fun, but why didn't he just mosey on down the trail. Tell him she didn't want him anymore.

Damn, he thought, running his hand down his face. He had to leave. He had to pack up and go before he lost himself totally to the silken web Cassidy was weaving around him. But to leave now was to take with him the unanswered questions of what was causing the unknown emotions about Cassidy to churn within him. Unanswered questions. Lord, he hated them. It had taken him years to quiet the ones that had plagued him before. Why had his mother deserted him without even a word of good-bye? Why had his father sought solace in a bottle instead of turning to his frightened and lonely son? Why had his father struck out physically at him, a boy who wanted only to be loved?

No. No more questions to weigh him down, Sagan decided firmly. When he left Cherokee, he would be free again, once he figured out and dismissed the strange hold Cassidy had on him. He wouldn't stay, because Sagan Jones didn't stay anywhere for long. It was safer that way. He always walked away before he could be told he wasn't wanted.

Fine.

But the very thought of leaving Cassidy brought the chill of emptiness back, twisting within him like the cold, ruthless blade of a knife.

Good Lord, what was happening to him?

"Cassidy," he said, getting quickly to his feet.

"Yes?"

"I . . . I'll pour the coffee, okay?"

"Sure." She frowned as she saw him wipe a line of sweat off his brow with his thumb. "Are you all right?"

"What? Oh, yeah, I'm fine. Ready to play bartender."

"Where did you learn to tend bar?" she asked, sliding the large omelet onto a plate.

"Here and there," he said, filling two mugs with coffee. "I've worked construction, driven an eighteen-wheeler, been a bouncer . . . All kinds of great stuff."

"Beaver said in a letter that there isn't much to do on oil-drilling sites, so he's finishing his college business degree by correspondence. He has a streak of wanderlust in him, like our parents. That's how he ended up being an oil driller. Did you ever take correspondence courses while you were overseas?"

Sagan nodded. "Yes. Most of the guys on the crew do. It fills the hours."

"Sit," Cassidy said, motioning toward the table. "Everything is ready." He settled onto his chair again, and Cassidy sat opposite him. "What kind of courses did you take?"

"Accounting," he said, filling his plate. "Business management. Some architecture. I drew up plans for a house that you wouldn't believe. Then, for the lack of anything better to do, I figured out what it would cost me to build it, doing most of the work myself."

"Are you going to? Build the house?"

"No."

"Why not?"

"I don't need a house like that. It's too big, has four bedrooms, and . . . No, I'll never build it. I was just killing time. I wasn't in the social hot spots of the world, you know. There was always a poker game going with the guys, but that gets old. I've seen Beaver studying. I wouldn't be surprised if he came home soon. I don't think he's cut out for the isolation that job forces on a man."

"But *you* were."

"It suited me just fine."

"Until now."

Sagan shrugged and went back to his meal. They ate in silence for several minutes. Then Cassidy looked at him again.

"Don't you want roots, Sagan? A home, a place where you know you belong?"

Yes, dammit! he screamed silently. Just once, just once in his life, he'd like to know how it felt to have those things. But it was dangerous—didn't she see that? If he let his guard down, reached out for those things, they could be whisked away beyond his fingertips.

"Sagan?"

"More coffee?" he asked, getting to his feet.

"No, thank you," Cassidy said. He hadn't answered her. He'd looked at a spot in the middle of her forehead and asked her if she wanted more coffee. "Sagan, when you first came here you said you'd quit your job because you *did* want roots, a sense of permanence. Have you changed your mind?"

He said down once more and frowned. "You're doing your CIA bit again."

"No, I'm not. I'm interested, that's all."

"Look, it's not that easy. I've been rambling around for as long as I can remember. Yeah, I quit my job with the idea that I wanted to settle down in one spot but . . ." His voice trailed off.

"But?" Cassidy asked, leaning slightly toward him.

"Well, if you told a man who had always lived a very structured existence that he suddenly had to move around continually, it would probably throw him off. The same goes for me. I know I want to settle down in one spot, but this little voice in my head says, 'Oh, yeah, Jones, just how do you intend to do that?' Hell, I don't *know* how to do it. Get the picture?"

Cassidy frowned. "I'm not sure. If you want to stay, you just don't leave. Sounds simple enough to me."

"And do what for a living?"

"Whatever you want. Building houses, doing accounting, tending bar," she said. At Illusions. With her. Sagan had a multitude of choices. He just didn't see that yet.

"Mmm," he said, frowning as he took a ·bite of omelet.

Dear heaven, Cassidy thought, she suddenly *did* understand what he was saying about not really knowing how to change his lifestyle. And it went even further than that.

Sagan Jones didn't know how to love.

And why should he? she asked herself. He'd never known love, not even as a little boy. He wouldn't recognize it if it hit him with a brick. He knew he felt new and strange emotions for her, but for all his worldliness it had probably never occurred to him that he might be falling in love with her. He had no frame of reference for that emotion. None at all.

Was it true? Could it be possible that Sagan did indeed love her? And if he figured out that he did, how would he feel about it? *And* how would he feel about Cassidy's love for *him*? So many questions. But the biggest question of all was, how did she fight for him? How did she show him how much, how very much, they could have together, share together, here in Cherokee? She really didn't know. But, darn it, she was going to find out. She was fighting for his love—fighting for her life.

"It's getting late," Cassidy said. "I'll clean up the kitchen, then shower."

"I'll do the kitchen," Sagan said. "You cooked, I'll clean. Go ahead and get ready for work."

"Well . . ."

"Go on."

"Okay," she said, getting to her feet. "Sagan?"

"Yes?"

"Thank you for a lovely day. It was . . . Well, thank you."

Their eyes met and held; then Sagan extended his hand toward her. Cassidy went around the table to place her hand in his, immediately feeling the heat travel up her arm and across her breasts with what felt like gently stroking fingers. She offered no resistance when he tugged on her hand, and in the next instant she was nestled on his lap, watching desire radiate from the deep, dark pools of his eyes.

He dipped his head slowly toward hers, but for Cassidy it was too slow, the waiting pure agony. She shifted slightly to sink her fingers into his thick damp hair, and urged his mouth to hers.

Sagan kissed her. Hungrily, he claimed her lips, then met her tongue as one arm circled her waist. His free hand roamed over her hip, then down her leg, skimming up again to cup the apex of her thighs, which throbbed with heated desire. He groaned deeply as she moved closer to his hand.

Cassidy was awash with heightened sensations, feeling, tasting, inhaling Sagan's aroma. His arousal was full, heavy, pressing against her, promising the ecstasy she knew he could bring to her. His hand increased its pressure, bringing a whimper from her throat.

Sagan lifted his head, then trailed nibbling kisses down her neck as he left her heated core to skim his hand under her sweater and fondle her breast.

"Oh, Sagan." She gave a soft sigh of pleasure.

"I'll never," he said, his voice raspy, "get enough of you. I ache with wanting you, Cassidy."

"Yes. Yes, I want you, too."

"There isn't time. We have to get to Illusions."

"There's time, if we hurry."

He chuckled softly. "Are you suggesting a quickie Miss Cole?"

"I am, Mr. Jones."

"Shame on you."

"Pshaw. Love me, Sagan." She sucked gently on his lower lip and felt his entire body tense. "Here. Right here," she murmured. "Make love to me."

"In the kitchen?" he asked, his breathing rough as he stroked her breast.

"I adore kitchens," she said, then traced his lips with the tip of her tongue. "No, I guess that's dumb. I don't think making love in the sink appeals to me."

"This kitchen will do just fine."

"Oh?"

"Mmm."

Within moments Sagan had removed her sweater and bra, then slid her jeans, panties, and shoes away without taking her off his lap. He lifted her by the waist and turned her toward him so that she was straddling his strong thighs, his hands traveling over her flowing hair and moist skin. He caught her mouth with his and plunged his tongue deep within it.

The faded denim of Sagan's jeans rubbing against her excited Cassidy even more, and with trembling fingers she unbuttoned his shirt, her hands sliding over the damp, curly chest hair and taut muscles beneath. She could feel Sagan's arousal straining against his jeans, and moved her hips sensuously back and forth over the heated ridge.

"Easy," he said as a shudder ripped through him, "or it's going to be too late. Damn, I want you. Don't move for a minute, Cassidy."

"But—"

"Don't—oh, Lord—move," he said, striving for control. "I can't believe what you do to me. I feel like a kid who . . . But, oh, damn, you're so beautiful, so passionate, so . . . Ah, hell," he said, then drew a taut nipple into his mouth.

"Oh, Sagan," she whispered, closing her eyes to savor the delicious sensations spiraling through her. She moved against him again, and he groaned.

He tore his mouth from her breast and spoke close to her lips. "Do you trust me?"

"Yes. Yes, of course."

He took possession of her mouth in a kiss so searing, it seemed to steal the very breath from her body. She felt Sagan's hand move between their bodies, heard the rasp of the zipper on his jeans. His hands slid to her buttocks, and then . . .

"Oh, Sagan!"

He thrust deep within her, causing a burst of colors to dance before her eyes. Gripping her hips, he began to move her, and she quickly matched his tempo as his strong body lifted to meet her. They thundered toward the summit of their climb, their labored breathing echoing in the quiet room.

"Sagan!"

"Yes. Take it all. I'm holding you. You're safe with me, Cassidy."

"Come with me, Sagan. Come . . . Oh!"

She arched her back as the glorious spasms swept through her, and called his name as she felt him lift himself once more to drive deep, so deep, within her. Shudders racked him, and even in her hazy mist of passion Cassidy knew he had joined her in their special, private place.

She went limp, falling against his chest, where she was caught by the steel bands of his arms. She buried her face in his neck as she clung to him, gasping for breath. Seconds passed into minutes, but neither spoke or moved.

"Dear . . . Lord," Sagan finally said, "that was incredible. *You* are incredible. Lord, Lord, Lord."

Cassidy slowly lifted her head to meet his gaze. "It was . . . Oh, my goodness."

"You really do trust me, don't you?" he asked, frowning slightly.

"Yes. Yes, I do."

He wove his fingers through her hair. "But you didn't know what I was going to do, that I was going to take you right here, like this. Weren't you frightened, Cassidy?"

"No, Sagan. That's what trust"—and love—"is all about."

"Incredible," he repeated, shaking his head.

He cupped her head with his large hands to bring her lips to his in a long, powerful kiss, then slowly, gently lifted her off him and onto her feet. He stood and adjusted his clothes as she scooped hers off the floor.

"I don't think," he said, fiddling with the buttons on his shirt instead of looking at her, "that anyone has ever really trusted me before."

"Maybe you never gave them a chance. You probably never gave anyone a glimpse of you, the real you, let people get close enough to trust you, know you."

"Maybe you're right," he said quietly, meeting her gaze. "No, I know you're right. But why? Why is everything so damn different with you? What are you doing to me, Cassidy?"

Loving you, Sagan, her mind whispered.

"Did it ever occur to you, Sagan," she said softly, "that it's time for *you* to trust someone?" And love someone. Her. "I'll shower and get dressed." She turned and left the kitchen.

Sagan watched her go, then raked restless fingers through his hair, noting with disgust that his hands were shaking. He began to clean up the kitchen, giving little thought to his task.

Trust someone? his mind echoed. Trust Cassidy? That was what she had really been saying. She'd been asking him to trust her. To do what? Cut him off at the knees when she tired of him, when she didn't want him anymore? She already had too much power over his body, his mind. But *she* trusted *him*. God in heaven, she really did. Her trust was a gift, a precious, fragile gift, the likes of which he'd never received before. There, in that kitchen, she had placed herself, her well-being, the very essence of all she was, in his care. This time their lovemaking had been different from that in the gentle, whimsical setting of the field of wild flowers. Cassidy could have felt that what had happened there in the kitchen was rough, coarse, cheap. But she hadn't, because she trusted him. Incredible.

But trust *her*? he asked himself. No, he . . . Or did he? He had told her more about himself than he'd ever revealed to another living soul. No one but Cassidy knew of his cold, empty childhood. No one but Cassidy knew that he was questioning his ability to settle into the life he so desperately sought. No one but Cassidy knew that despite his cool outer facade he was floundering, searching for his place, a sense of purpose and direction. The words had flowed from him as easily as a summer rain. He had told her his thoughts as they came to him . . . because he trusted her.

"I'll be damned," he said, wiping off the table. Probably not the brightest thing he'd ever done, he decided, but he did trust Cassidy. It was scary as hell, yet at the same time it was warming, flowing through him like rich brandy, taking some of the edge off the chill within him. He was definitely asking for trouble, setting himself up for a hard, heavy fall. Well, too late . . . he trusted her.

So what was next? he wondered. What part of him did she sew up tightly next? Well, this trust stuff wasn't so bad. It was nice, really nice, to have someone to talk to, someone who listened, who at least tried to understand him. In fact, he could live with this—Cassidy's trusting him, his trusting Cassidy. But what was next? He had absolutely no idea. There were more emotions churning inside him, but at least now one had a name. Trust.

"Sagan?" Cassidy called from the living room. "Are you ready to go?"

"Uh-oh," he said, picking up the dirty frying pan. He stuck it in the oven. "All set." He went into the living room, automatically stepping around Mrs. Henderson's plants. Then he stopped, his eyes widening. "What in the—" His gaze raked over Cassidy, a frown deepening on his face as he took in every inch of her. "No," he said, shaking his head. "Absolutely not. No way. No."

"What are you blithering about?"

"Go change your clothes," he said, folding his arms over his chest.

"What?"

"You heard me. Whatever that thing is, you're not wearing it."

"What! This 'thing' happens to be a duplicate of an authentic Hawaiian hula skirt and halter. If you weren't such a stick in the mud, you could be wearing Barry's nifty flowered shirt and the lei."

"Dammit, Cassidy," Sagan roared, "your stomach is bare, your breasts are poking above the top of that thing, your hair is loose, and . . . There, see? You moved. I saw your thighs beneath that grass. Go change," he ordered, pointing to the bedroom.

"I certainly will not. I wear this every Saturday night. What are you pitching such a fit about?"

"Are you nuts? Do you have any idea how sexy you look? Dammit, Cassidy, no one sees your thighs, your breasts, your hair loose, but me," he said, thumping himself on the chest. "I won't have a bunch of guys ogling you."

"Ogling?" She burst into laughter. "That's a great word."

"Go change!"

"No!"

Sagan narrowed his eyes and started slowly toward her. Cassidy felt the color drain from her face, but she stood her ground, lifting her chin in what she hoped was a determined, defiant gesture. Sagan stopped in front of her, towering above her with a thunderous expression on his face.

"My customers and friends"—Oh, damn, her voice was squeaking—"do not ogle."

"Ha!"

"They don't. They don't touch, either. Mitzy and Carmen wear outfits just like this on Saturday. Sat-

urday is Hawaiian day, Mr. Jones. I have no intention of changing my clothes."

Sagan shifted his gaze to the ceiling as he reined
in his raging temper. "The first man," he said through
clenched teeth, "who ogles, gets a busted jaw."

"Fine," she replied, spinning around and starting
toward the door. "Terrific. Then your old buddy Harry
the sheriff can toss you in the clink."

"Big deal. I've been in jail before."

"Somehow that doesn't surprise me," she said as
she flung open the door.

"Cassidy."

"Now what?" she snapped.

Sagan's voice was low-pitched and quiet when he
spoke. "I've been in my share of fights, but never
over a woman. But I swear, I won't stand silently by
and watch anyone touch, even with his eyes, what is
mine. And you *are* mine, Cassidy. If you think that
sounds too possessive, too chauvinistic, that's tough,
because that's how it is. While I'm here in Cherokee
you're my lady, my woman. Mine. Understand? Do
you have a problem with that?"

You'd better believe I do, Jones, she silently fumed.
Just who in the blazes did he think he was? What
nerve! What gall! Talk about award-winning ma-
chismo. Sagan Jones was living in the wrong de-
cade, the wrong century. What a pushy, arrogant
so-and-so. Oh, she wished she weighed two hundred pounds so she could punch him in the nose.
His woman? Baloney. She—

"Cassidy?"

"No, Sagan," she said softly, "I have no problem
with that at all."

"Good." He nodded decisively. "Let's go."

Being in love, Cassidy decided glumly, was turning her brain into oatmeal. It was also absolutely glorious. Never before had she felt so protected, so cherished and cared for. Sagan's words poured through her like sunshine on a summer day, leaving not one inch of room for the chill of loneliness.

Sagan drove Cassidy's car to Illusions, declaring that at least in Harry's Jeep there was room for a man's knees.

"Knobby knees," Cassidy said, smiling sweetly. Sagan glared at her.

Inside the club, Cassidy turned on the lights and immediately went to check the liquor stock behind the bar. Sagan wandered into the storeroom, then into the room next to it. The second room was empty, except for a dozen large boxes stacked against the wall.

"There's a lot of wasted space here," he called out.

"It's not wasted if there's nothing to use it for," Cassidy said, coming to the doorway.

"What's in the boxes?"

"Cans of peanuts. There used to be three times that many."

"Why would you want so many peanuts?"

She pressed one finger to her chin. "It was very strange how that happened."

Sagan chuckled. "Here we go again."

"Well, this trucker came through—actually, he was lost—and it was his birthday. So he ordered drinks for everyone in Illusions. Then another round of drinks, and another. Barry had to carry the poor guy to the cab of the truck to sleep it off. Anyway, the next day the trucker realized that he didn't have any money. So—"

"He gave you peanuts instead."

"Yep. About a zillion, I'd say. We're getting to the point where we have to plead with people to eat them."

"You're unreal," Sagan said, smiling. "But this room," he went on, "would be perfect."

"What for?"

"Making sandwiches and desserts. Let's see. Add a sink there, a couple of refrigerators, a stove, a freezer, tables, shelves . . . Perfect. Of course, you'd have to apply for a food-handling license."

"We have one."

"You're kidding."

Cassidy laughed. "Nope. The inspector who came from Jasper said he never again intended to drive over those mountains. So he issued a liquor license and a food-handling license at the same time. Barry and I had gotten health cards already. Mitzy and Carmen would need them to serve food, but . . ." She shrugged. "Oh, well, no matter. We're not going to do it, anyway."

"Why not?"

"I told you. It would mean extra hours, and hiring someone, and . . . It's too much of a hassle. We're doing fine just the way we are."

"Mmm."

"Meaning?"

"Meaning," he said, shoving his hands into his back pockets, "that it may be fine for you, but what about Barry? He's about to become a father. He's got to think about financial security for that child. Things like braces on teeth, college, permanents."

"Permanents?"

"Well, if it's a girl, they like to have fancy hairdos, and junk."

"Oh, I see," she said with a smile.

"I'm serious, Cassidy. You're not tapping the full potential of this place. After that baby gets here, you and Barry should sit down and discuss this. In fact . . . Well, I'm overstepping myself."

"No, you're not. What were you going to say?"

"Just that I know about accounting, cost analysis, all that jazz. If I could see your books, I could give you a pretty clear picture of what it would cost to expand. Then all you and Barry would have to do is read my report and make a decision."

"I couldn't ask you to do all that, Sagan."

"I'd enjoy it. I had a great time figuring out how much it would cost to build that house I'm never going to build."

"Well, I guess you do have hours to fill while you're waiting for your belongings to catch up with you."

"My what? Oh. Yes. Of course. Right. Yep, no telling where all that stuff is. So it's settled? I'll work up a report for you?"

"I should ask Barry, I suppose. No, forget that. He has enough on his mind. It's not as though I'm making a major decision without him. Okay, Sagan, you figure it all out. Oh, look at the time. I've got to open up. Saturday is our busiest night."

"For oglers?" Sagan asked, flexing his right hand.

"Oh, stop it, Mr. Macho." Cassidy laughed. "The male residents of Cherokee are gentlemen, one and all."

"Mmm."

Cassidy rolled her eyes to the heavens.

• • •

Two hours later, Sagan began to relax. Illusions was packed to overflowing, the band was playing, and not one man had ogled his Cassidy. She might as well be wearing a gunnysack, for all the attention they were paying her. Were these guys blind? he wondered. Didn't they realize what a vision of loveliness Cassidy was? Mitzy and Carmen weren't hard on the eyes, either, in their hula outfits, but they weren't getting any lewd leers. Interesting. These were rought-cut blue-collar men, but they treated the three women with the respect due them. That was fine with him. It had no doubt saved him from having a busted hand.

"Hi, sweetie."

"Hello, love of my life," Sagan said to Aunt Patty. "Cherry Coke?"

"With two cherries. Cassidy, did you hear from Barry?"

"No," Cassidy said. "I hope he calls tomorrow. I'm anxious to know how Barbie is."

A short, heavily muscled man came into the bar, flanked by two taller but equally well-built men.

"Hi, Chunky," Cassidy greeted him. "Wilbur, Joe Peter." She smiled at the other two.

"There you go, Aunt Patty." Sagan handed her a glass. "That's on me. I owe you one."

"You do?" Cassidy asked. "Why?"

"I'll pay for it myself." Sagan was digging into his pocket. "There."

"Why?" Cassidy asked again.

"None of your business, nosy girl," Aunt Patty told her. "Sagan and I have private doings."

"Well, excuse me," Cassidy said. She paused. "Really? What kind of doings?"

"Private," Aunt Patty said. "Chunky, go home. Take Wilbur and Joe Peter and go. Right now. Shoo."

Chunky laughed. "I'm thirty years old now, Aunt Patty. I get to stay up later than when you used to baby-sit me."

"Chunky, please," Aunt Patty was very serious. "Go home, the three of you."

"Oh, Lord," Cassidy whispered. "They're here, aren't they? Aunt Patty? Did you see them? Did they come over from Jasper? All five?"

"What in the hell is going on?" Sagan asked.

Aunt Patty sighed. "They're here. They're fixing a flat down at the garage."

"Who?" Sagan asked.

"Damn their hides," Chunky said. "Don't worry, Cassidy, we'll meet them outside. We won't tear up your place, like the other time."

"Okay, that's it." Sagan smacked the bar with his hand. "What's this all about?"

"The McKinney brothers," Cassidy said, feeling the color drain from her face. "They hate Chunky, Wilbur, and Joe Peter because they danced with the McKinney sisters at a dance in Jasper. Cherokee men are not supposed to mess around with Jasper women, and vice versa. It's all so dumb. Oh, Sagan, the McKinney brothers are huge. They fight dirty, too, with knives and . . . Chunky, Wilbur, Joe Peter, go home."

"Amen to that," Aunt Patty said. "Shoo."

The door to Illusions swung open.

"Too late." Aunt Patty shook her head. "They're here."

"No joke," Sagan remarked, looking at the five men. "They're mountains."

"Oh, Lord, Sagan," Cassidy said. "What are we going to do?"

Sagan flexed his right hand again. "I knew I was saving this for something. We'll even the odds a little, Chunky."

"No, Sagan," Chunky said. "This is our fight. There's a dozen guys in this place who would help us if we asked, but we won't. It's a matter of honor."

"And I respect that," Sagan said, nodding. "But, Chunky, those jokers just brought trouble inside Illusions, and Illusions is Cassidy's, and Cassidy is mine."

The two men looked at each other for a long moment as Cassidy wrung her hands and chewed nervously on her bottom lip. A smile broke across Chunky's face.

"Then let's give 'em hell, Sagan," he said.

"Oh, dear Lord," Cassidy whispered, pressing her shaking fingers to her lips. "Oh, Sagan, no."

Seven

Amazing, Sagan thought. Never in his life had he seen a place, especially a bar, become so quiet so fast. The band had stopped playing, no one was speaking, all eyes were riveted on the scene at the door.

"Been looking for you and your buddies, Chunky," the largest McKinney brother said. "We got unfinished business."

"Take it outside," Sagan said.

"Oh, yeah?" another McKinney challenged. "Says who? Stay out of this. It ain't none of your affair."

"It is now," Sagan told him. "You made it my business when you brought it inside my lady's bar."

"Club," Cassidy said absently, her eyes darting between Sagan and the five big men.

"Cassidy is yours?" another brother asked. His eyes raked slowly over Cassidy. "I was wondering who was going to get that sweet stuff into bed."

"I don't think he should have said that," Cassidy

said under her breath. Every muscle in Sagan's body was tense. "Oh, Lord."

"Haul it out of here," Sagan said through clenched teeth. "You ogle her again like that, buster, and I'm going to take you apart."

A hysterical giggle escaped from Cassidy's lips. "He probably doesn't know what ogle means."

"You and what army?" the McKinney asked with a sneer. "Maybe we ought to put up Cassidy as the prize for this go-round. I'd like a chance to get my hands on that pretty hair. Must look good spread out over a pillow just before a man drops his—"

Sagan moved so fast that Cassidy saw hardly more than a blur of motion. One moment he was next to her behind the bar, and in the next instant he was flying through the air. Using the bar top as a diving board, he flew at the five McKinney brothers, crashing to the floor with his arms wrapped around the necks of two of them.

It was bedlam.

Cassidy screamed and pressed her hands to her cheeks.

Chunky, Wilbur, and Joe Peter launched themselves at the remaining McKinneys, fists flying.

"Hot damn, we've got 'em this time!" Aunt Patty crowed.

The other customers were on their feet, cheering on their friends.

It was grunts and groans as fists connected, four-letter words rang out, bodies moved in a blend of color and straining muscles. A table collapsed when a McKinney landed on it with a sickening thud. The crowd moved back to clear the dance floor as the pitched battle spread farther into the room. Cassidy saw Sagan double over as he took a vicious blow to the stomach.

"Sagan!" she yelled, running out from behind the bar.

"Stay back, Cassidy," he ordered, then delivered a right cross to the McKinney in front of him.

"Keep out of the way, Cassidy," Aunt Patty said. "Our boys are doing fine, just fine. 'Bout time we showed those McKinney creeps what for. Sagan sure knows how to handle himself in a fight. Land's sake, he's quick. Oh! Did you see that? He broke a McKinney nose, I'd bet on it."

"I'm thrilled," Cassidy said dryly. "This has to stop. I can't stand it. I'm calling the sheriff."

"No sense in that," Aunt Patty said. "I saw Harry just before I came in here. He said it was time this was settled once and for all, and with Sagan here looking out for you, the fight would be evened up some. He said he'd drop by later."

"Wonderful," Cassidy muttered. "Some sheriff he is. Oh, Lord, Sagan's mouth is bleeding. His eye is bleeding. Everyone is bleeding."

"Hush," Aunt Patty said. "A little blood never hurt anyone."

Another table was smashed to smithereens.

"Hey!" Cassidy said. "That's my property you're destroying there, you hoodlums."

A McKinney lay unmoving in the debris of the table. Then two McKinneys were down for the count. The fight went on and on. Three, then four McKinneys toppled over with a groan and didn't move.

Then Illusions became deathly quiet.

In the center of the dance floor, Sagan was breathing heavily, as was the McKinney a few feet from him. It was the one who had made the lewd remarks about Cassidy, and Sagan's face was a mask of raw fury.

In the McKinney brother's hand was a gleaming knife.

"Oh, Lord. Oh, no," Cassidy said. "Chunky, do something. Please."

"Can't," Chunky said, sagging against the bar. "There's honor at stake here, Cassidy. That scum said lousy things about you, and you're Sagan's lady. This is their fight now. We've finished ours."

"Dammit, Chunky, he has a knife."

"Sagan can take care of himself. Can I have a beer?"

"Get it yourself," Cassidy said. "Oh, merciful heaven, would you look at that knife? Oh, Sagan, please be careful."

"Hush, hush," Aunt Patty said. "Sagan has to concentrate."

Sagan drew a deep breath into his burning lungs, stalling for time as he took stock of his enemy. His gaze was riveted on the face of the huge man before him, rather than on the knife in his hand. Sagan knew from experience that the man's eyes would warn him of an attack seconds before the wicked blade came slicing through the air. The two circled each other slowly, very slowly. It was still deathly quiet.

Sagan wiped the back of his hand over his eye to clear his vision. It was wet with blood when he pulled it away. His eye was swelling. Lip was split. No big deal. But, oh, damn, the pain in his chest said he had a cracked or broken rib. That was a pretty big deal. Another solid punch in the wrong spot, and he was liable to pass out cold on his face. He had to take this sleazeball out . . . fast.

"Brought your Tinker Toy, I see," Sagan taunted him. "I'm not impressed, McKinney. A real man fights fair. But then, you're not a real man, are you?"

A collective gasp went up from the crowd.

"I'm going to kill you," McKinney snarled.

"Kill?" Chunky whispered, his eyes widening. "Who said anything about killing? There're rules about this stuff. Where in the hell is the sheriff?"

"Go find him," Aunt Patty ordered. "Dear Lord, this has gotten out of hand."

Sagan! Cassidy's mind screamed. It didn't matter that McKinney had ogled her. Ogling was harmless. Knives were not. Damn that Sagan Jones. If he got himself killed, she'd be so furious, she'd never speak to him again. This whole thing was crazy. It had to stop. Oh, Sagan, please. Please.

"What are you waiting for, McKinney?" Sagan asked, still circling the big man. "Nervous? Afraid you'll find that knife in your gut, instead of mine? Ever been cut, McKinney? Know what it feels like when that blade slices through your body?"

"Shut up!" the man bellowed.

Now!

Sagan lunged forward at the exact moment when the knife slashed through the air. Sagan felt the hot white flash of pain and swore silently as he slammed into the last McKinney. They crashed to the floor. The knife was jarred loose and slid across the dance floor, where Carmen planted her foot firmly on top of it. Sagan raised his fist and pulled it back.

"Don't ever ogle my Cassidy again," he said, then

delivered a stunning blow to McKinney's jaw. The man went limp beneath him.

The silence in Illusions was broken only by the sound of Sagan's labored breathing. With a groan he pushed himself to his feet, weaving unsteadily as blood soaked through his ripped shirt and onto his jeans. The crowd came out of its stupor, and a wild cheer of approval reverberated through the building.

"Sagan," Cassidy said, tears misting her eyes. She ran forward, flinging herself into his arms, then stepped back quickly as he moaned from the impact. "Oh, Sagan. Oh, Lord, Sagan, you're bleeding and . . . Sagan, speak to me."

"Hello," he said, smiling crookedly. "Good-bye," he added, then crumpled in a heap at her feet.

He was a dying man, Sagan thought foggily. He hurt. Lord, he hurt; every bone and muscle in his body hurt. His hair hurt, even his toe. Yeah, he had a sore toe, just like the rooster. What rooster? Hell, he didn't know. Where was he? He didn't know that either. He was on some oil-drilling site in a Godforsaken place, he supposed. If he opened his eyes he might have a clue, but his eyes hurt, so forget that. He was dying, anyway, so what difference did it make where he was?

He groaned. A dying man ought to groan a little, he decided. It seemed like the thing to do. What had happened to him? His mind was fuzzy. From the way he felt, he must have been hit by a train, or had an oil rig fall on him. Lord, what a stupid thing to do. He wasn't even going to croak with class.

He groaned again, more loudly.

"Sagan?"

Holy Toledo, he mentally mumbled, what a voice. An angel had called his name. Brother, had she made a mistake. Sagan Jones was no candidate for the gates of heaven. But what a sweet voice.

"Sagan? Can you hear me? Please, Sagan, open your eyes."

The angel was a bit of a nag, he mused. What did she want with him? To check his ID? She'd find out she had the wrong Sagan Jones, and ship him off in the other direction. Hell, no, he wasn't going to open his eyes.

"No."

"Sagan, please. The doctor gave you a shot for the pain, but you've been asleep so long, and I'm so worried. Please wake up, just for a minute, so I can be sure that you're all right. Then you can go back to sleep, okay?"

Oh-h-h, that poor little angel, Sagan thought fuzzily. She sounded so sad. Angels shouldn't be sad. There were tears in her voice now. Maybe he'd better open his eyes. If he could. They were heavy, had bricks on them and—

"Sagan, it's Cassidy." She choked on a sob. "I can't stand seeing you lying there so still for all these hours. Oh, Sagan, please. I love you. I need to know you're all right. Sagan?"

What? Who? Cassidy? And she loved him? That was nuts. Nobody loved Sagan Jones. Cassidy. Cassidy. Who . . . ? Good Lord, Cassidy! Cherokee. Illusions. The McKinney creeps. He hadn't been hit by a train; he'd been in a fight. Cassidy loved him? She did? No, she didn't. She did? Oh-h-h, his head hurt.

"Oh-h-h," Sagan groaned. "Waffirdy?"

"Yes. Yes, it's me. Can you open your eyes? Well, one, anyway. The other one is swollen nearly shut. Try, okay? Please?"

Sure thing. "Thur thin," he mumbled, then slowly, painfully opened his eyes a fraction of an inch. How's that? "House sat?"

Cassidy placed her hand on his cheek. "Hello, my Sagan," she said softly. "I'm so glad to see you."

He turned his head in the direction of her voice. "Oh-h-h. Hell. Damn." His vision cleared slightly, and there she was. Cassidy. She loved him? No, he'd imagined the part where she'd said that. Hadn't he? No, he really didn't think he had imagined it. " 'Lo," he said.

"Hi," she said, smiling as she dashed the tears from her cheeks.

"What . . . Where . . . Hell."

"It's Sunday afternoon, Sagan. You've been asleep for hours and hours. We took you to the clinic, and the doctor stitched up the knife wound and taped your ribs. He gave you a shot of a powerful pain-killer, and said you didn't have to go to the hospital in Jasper as long as you stayed quiet. You're in bed in my apartment. I should have left you alone, I guess, but I needed to assure myself that you were really going to wake up. Well, um, go back to sleep."

"Oh," he said. Had all that made sense? Yeah, it had. "Water."

"Of course," she said. She slid her arm under his shoulders, then reached for a glass on the night-stand. "Up you go."

"Oh-h-h."

"Easy. Drink it slowly."

Sagan drained the glass, and Cassidy lowered him back against the pillow. He lifted his hands and pressed them against his throbbing temples.

"What kind of shot did that jerk give me?"

"I don't know. Something for the pain. You're awfully battered. You have a cracked rib, and the knife . . . Oh, Sagan, I was so scared. The knife, the blood, the . . . I hated it."

"Hey," he said. He fumbled around for her hand, but couldn't find it. "I'm fine. Really. The fog is lifting, and I can tell that I feel worse from the shot than from what the McKinneys dished out. Man, what a fight, huh?"

"What?" she said, stiffening in her chair.

"Really got the old adrenaline flowing."

Cassidy got slowly to her feet. "You"—she took a deep breath—"are the most despicable, the most rotten, man on the face of the earth. How could you have enjoyed that bloody brawl? I've been out of my mind with worry. You're nothing but a little boy masquerading in a muscle-bound, grown-up body. I hope your other eye swells up. I hope everything that hurts . . . falls off."

He frowned. "That's not very nice. Especially considering the various parts of my anatomy that hurt."

"Don't speak to me."

"What's wrong with you? A minute ago you were an angel. Now, you're screaming at me. I'm a veteran of a battle fought to protect your honor. Where's your sympathy? What happened to the old 'kiss it and make it better' routine? Geez, some angel you are. What's for dinner?"

"Oh, I'm going to murder you," she said, squinting at him. "I'm going to strangle you with my bare hands. Do you have any idea what I've been through? I have never in my life seen so much blood, and you didn't move. You didn't move, Sagan." Tears spilled onto her cheeks. "I thought you were going to die, and I couldn't bear it. You were going to die before I'd told you that I love you, and my heart was breaking because you'd never hold me, or kiss me again, or . . . Oh, go to hell." She spun around and marched toward the door. "I hate you, Sagan!"

"Cassidy!" he yelled. "Oh-h-h." He clutched his head. His arms fell to the bed with a thud, and he closed his eyes. Somehow he'd blown it. Women were very confusing creatures. They were soft, smelled good, had the ability to take a man to heaven itself, but they were definitely confusing. Now Cassidy hated him? He was just getting used to the idea that she loved him.

Did she? he wondered. Love him? Really love him, as in a woman being in love with her man? What if she did? How did he feel about that? If he didn't have such a lousy headache, he might be able to figure it out. Sleep. He needed sleep. When he woke up, he'd sort this all through.

He moaned once more for good measure, then fell asleep.

Cassidy sat on the grass in the courtyard, her back against a tree, arms folded over her breasts, lips pursed. Never in her whole life had she been so angry. She wanted Sagan out of her bed and out of her life. No, she didn't. She hated him. No, she didn't. She loved him with every breath in her body.

Yes, she did. And for two cents she'd stick him on the next bus for Jasper. No, she wouldn't.

Cassidy sniffled, then looked up as Aunt Patty came out of the back door of the apartment and walked across the grass. She lowered herself to the ground beside Cassidy.

"Your front door was unlocked," Aunt Patty said. "I brought some dinner for you and Sagan. I figured you'd be too worn out to cook. You look terrible. How's our boy? I peeked into the bedroom, and he seems to be sleeping like a baby."

"That boy," Cassidy said, frowning, "has decided that the fight with the McKinneys was the social event of the year."

"It was something, wasn't it?" Aunt Patty said merrily. "I'd bet twenty bucks that those McKinneys won't be back. Land's sake, our boys were tough. I'm just as proud as a peacock."

"I can't believe this," Cassidy said, throwing up her hands. "What about the knife, the blood, the—Oh, forget it."

"I understand, honey," Aunt Patty said, patting Cassidy's knee. "Sagan looked as though he was about to draw his last breath. I was a bit shook up myself for a moment, there. I'm sure it was harder on you, seeing how you love him, and all."

"I do not," Cassidy said sullenly.

"Yes, you do."

"Yes, I do," Cassidy said with a sigh. "I wish I didn't, but I do. It's like everything else that happens to me. I'm in a terrible mess, and I'm not quite sure how I got there. But here I am, smack-dab in love with a man who doesn't love me and is only passing through town. Dumb, dumb, dumb."

"Mmm," Aunt Patty said.

"Don't make that Sagan Jones noise, Aunt Patty. I can't stand it."

Aunt Patty laughed. "You're coming unglued, Cassidy."

"That much I know. Speaking of the notorious Mr. Jones, are you going to tell me what this private business is you have with him?"

"Nope."

"Fine. I don't care."

"You're pouting, Cassidy. I'll give you some news that will cheer you up. In all the flurry last night, you didn't lock the door to Illusions. Chunky, Wilbur, Joe Peter, and at least a dozen others are over there right now cleaning up the place. Joe Peter is a whiz with a hammer and saw. He's making you new tables. The others are scrubbing and rubbing the whole shebang. You'll never know that the battle of Cherokee versus Jasper was fought in there."

"That's very nice of them," Cassidy said softly. "It really is."

"They're concerned about Sagan too. I said I'd stop back by and give them a report. They think mighty highly of Sagan, you know. He's all right, isn't he?"

"I think so. He said he felt worse from the shot than from anything else."

"He surely can handle himself in a fight. He's a tough cookie, but . . ."

"But?"

"There's a gentleness about him, too, Cassidy. A—How do you say it?—a vulnerability below the surface. I'd guess that Sagan has had a rough life. A life that maybe didn't have much loving in it. Oh, I don't know. Maybe I'm just a silly old lady talking through her hat. All I'm trying to say is, there's a lot more to Sagan than meets the eye. Be patient with him, Cassidy. And don't be so hard on yourself. You're in love, and I, for one, think you picked yourself a fine man."

"But he's leaving," Cassidy said with a wail. "As soon as he's better, as soon as his belongings arrive, as soon as he figures out what has him all in a dither about me, he's leaving. The bum."

"You never know what tomorrow will bring." Aunt Patty got to her feet. "Go take a nap. You'll feel more like yourself."

"Myself is miserable. Thank you for bringing the dinner, and thank Chunky and the others for what they're doing at Illusions."

"You betcha. I'll talk to you later."

" 'Bye, Aunt Patty."

Cassidy leaned her head back against the tree and closed her eyes with a weary sigh. She was tired, she realized. Bone tired. She'd had only snatches of sleep during the long hours of the night as she'd sat in the chair next to the bed watching Sagan. She was emotionally tired, too. Drained. Maybe if she had a nap she could view things more objectively. At the moment she was totally depressed.

Cassidy got to her feet and walked slowly back into the apartment. In the bedroom she stood by the edge of the bed and stared at the sleeping Sagan. He looked awful, she decided. He needed a shave, his eye and bottom lip were swollen, and he was various shades of black and blue. Beneath the blanket, she knew, he had a tight bandage encasing his ribs and an ugly row of a dozen stitches closing the knife wound. He was also stark naked, but she wasn't going to think about that.

He was, she thought with a sigh, beautiful, beautiful Sagan. And she loved him.

Cassidy went to the other side of the bed and slipped off her shoes before stretching out, not bothering to remove her jeans and T-shirt. Within moments she was deeply asleep, her hand resting on top of Sagan's.

Sagan stirred, considered groaning, decided he was tired of that routine, and opened his eyes. The room glowed with the golden luminescence of the sunset, and he realized that he'd slept the afternoon away. He also realized that there was a warm, soft hand on top of one of his rough ones. He turned his head, registered the fact that it didn't hurt, and saw Cassidy sleeping next to him. Beautiful, beautiful Cassidy.

His heart beat wildly as he gazed at her, seeing her luscious cascade of hair, her slightly parted, oh, so kissable lips, the fullness of her breasts, the feminine curves of her body. Cassidy. Cassidy, who had said that she loved him. She hated him at the same time, somehow, but she *had* said that she loved him.

So? he asked himself. How did he feel about it? How did he feel about the fact that Cassidy was in love with him? He didn't know. He didn't know what to do with it, where to put it, because no one had ever loved him before. Not ever. He didn't know what he should do or say to her about it, or what his responsibilities were. Oh, he'd had women declare their love for him, but it had always been in the heat of passion, and he'd ignored the thickly spoken words. But this was the real goods. Love. Cassidy loved him.

And he was shaken to the very recesses of his soul.

He was filled with the greatest fear and the greatest joy he'd ever known.

The feelings tumbled together within him—half heaven, half hell. Half warmth, half icy cold. Half peace, half turmoil. He wanted to stay; he wanted to flee. He wanted to laugh aloud from sheer happiness, and rage in anger in the next breath. He was being offered a precious gift, like none he'd ever had, and he didn't know how to keep from crushing it into dust. He didn't know how to be loved, or what was expected of him in return. But he was able to name more and more of the emotions twisting around inside him. There was also fear, and mind-boggling confusion.

What in the hell was he going to do? And what were the names of the other emotions that still hid in the shadows of his soul?

Questions. So many questions, and he had to find the answers. He had to, no longer only for himself, but for Cassidy's sake as well, because now she loved him.

As though sensing Sagan's heated, troubled gaze on her, Cassidy slowly lifted her lashes, her blue eyes meeting his dark ones.

"Hi," he said softly.

"Hello," she said, her voice husky with sleep. "How are you feeling?"

"Good as new."

"I somehow doubt that," she said, smiling slightly. "Goodness, I slept so long."

"You must have needed it. I guess I put you through a rough night. I'm sorry, Cassidy. I've been banged up before, but, well, there was only a bunch of roughnecks around, who let me sleep it off. No one has ever been particularly worried or upset. I really am sorry."

"Well, I'm sorry for yelling at you the way I did. It was new for me, too, Sagan, to be sick with worry, to have someone that I . . . someone so important to me hurt. I guess we were both in a situation we'd never been in before, and we didn't know how to react. That makes sense, I think."

"Yes, I think it does." He rolled carefully onto his side and filled one hand with the heavy silken weight of her hair. "Cassidy?"

"Yes?"

He looked directly into her eyes. "Did you mean it? When you said that you love me, did you mean it?"

What was the point of playing games? she asked herself. Why deny what was probably evident every time she looked at him, every time he touched her?

"Cassidy?"

"Yes, Sagan," she whispered, "I love you. I didn't mean to love you. It just happened. I know it doesn't change the fact that you'll be leaving Cherokee, but I don't know how to be anything but honest with you. I love you, Sagan, with all my heart."

Sagan squeezed his eyes tightly closed as a lump formed in his throat. Dear God, he thought incredulously, he was close to tears. They were burning behind his eyes, and his throat was tight and aching. He'd cried once, so very long ago, when his mother had left him. Those had been tears of sadness. This feeling, this emotion—what was its name? What was there, mingled with the fear and confusion, the joy and the anger?

Tenderness. Peace. Protectiveness toward Cassidy.

The urge to hold her and never let her go. A feeling of manliness beyond anything he'd experienced. A sense of completeness that warred with a lifetime of being alone. And the confusion and fear that demanded to be heard.

"I don't know what to say," he said, his voice oddly husky.

"I don't expect you to say anything. I really don't. It's mine to deal with, Sagan. It was never my intention to put any pressure on you or make you feel guilty. You should forget I even said it, if that's possible."

"I don't want to forget it. Listen to me, okay? I said no one had ever worried about me when I'd been hurt. Well, no one has ever loved me before, either."

"Oh, Sagan."

"Let me finish. I don't know how . . . Cassidy, I don't know how to be loved. I don't know what to say or do, or how to act. And I don't know how to figure out what it is that I'm feeling for you. I may never know any of these things, even though I'm trying so damn hard. It might be too late for me. Can you understand that?"

"Yes."

"I could hurt you, Cassidy. I could hurt you so damn much. There are parts of me, inside of me, that are frozen solid, ice cold. I don't know if I can change that. It's as though I'm holding your gift of love in my hands, and I don't know where to put it, what to do with it. I might crush it, destroy it, and along with it, you. Dammit, I don't want that to happen. I never want to hurt you, but I'm not sure I can stop it from happening."

"I understand, Sagan."

"Would it be better for you if I left Cherokee now?"

"No."

"You're sure?"

"I'm sure. I don't want to talk about this any more right now, Sagan, because I'll probably cry, and that wouldn't solve a thing. Aunt Patty brought us some dinner. I'll put it on a tray for you."

"I need a shower."

"You can't get those stitches wet. You could wash up, though. Then we'll eat. Oh, by the way, Chunky and a bunch of the others are fixing up Illusions."

"That's good. Great. I guess we really demolished the place. I'm glad they're cleaning it up. They're decent guys. Everyone in Cherokee is a cut above the herd. Fine, fine people, and they realize how special you are."

"They think highly of you, too, Sagan. Aunt Patty promised to go back by Illusions and tell them you were all right."

"No kidding. Really? I'll be damned." A smile spread across his face.

"That's new for you, too, isn't it? A whole group of people caring about you."

"Beats me why they should. They don't even know me."

"They know you, Sagan. I'm beginning to think

that the only person who doesn't know who you really are, is you."

"That's nuts."

"Think about it," she said, swinging her feet to the floor. "Do you need some help getting up?"

He gave a deep, throaty chuckle. "Miss Cole, that is a very provocative question."

She glared at him over her shoulder. "I didn't mean *that*."

"Never let it be said that Sagan Jones needed help getting up."

She burst into laughter, and felt the crimson flush on her cheeks. "You're naughty," she said, smiling. "You're also having delusions of grandeur, mister. You're battered, beat up, and bruised. Face it, Jones, you're temporarily out of commission."

"Oh, yeah?" He grabbed her arm and pulled her back onto the bed. He brought his lips close to hers. "Wanna bet? Let's check this out."

"Let's not," she said, her heart beating wildly. "The doctor said you had to be quiet."

"Check. I'll be quiet. I'll make love to you without saying a word."

"No!"

"And I won't groan with pleasure"—his voice was low and rumbly—"when I bury myself so deep inside you, and feel you tighten around me. I'll be as quiet as a mouse when I thrust, again and again, within you."

"Oh, dear Lord," Cassidy said as heated desire swirled within her.

He brushed his lips over hers. "But you, Cassidy, can make those sexy sounds, those whimpers, those moans. You can call my name with your angel voice, and we'll fly. Fly away. Together."

"Oh, yes," she said dreamily, her eyes drifting closed. An instant later her eyes popped back open. "No! You're crazy, Sagan. Your big activities for the evening are to wash up, then have some dinner. That's it."

"Well, hell."

She wriggled away from him and slid off of the bed. "I'm going to go see what Aunt Patty brought for dinner. In the meantime, you can concentrate on 'getting up.' Alone. It'll be a thrill a minute. Tally-ho." She waggled her fingers at him, and hurried from the room.

Sagan chuckled and sank back onto the pillow. "Ah, Cassidy," he said quietly, his smile fading, "you really are something." And he would have given everything he had, to know, to be guaranteed, that he wouldn't hurt her. That he wouldn't be the one to make her cry.

Eight

In the kitchen, Cassidy discovered a platter of fried chicken in the refrigerator, along with a bowl of fruit salad. Folding back the calico cloth on a basket on the table, she found a mound of flaky biscuits. After making a pot of coffee she set the table, deciding that stubborn Jones probably wouldn't behave himself and eat his dinner on a tray in bed.

"Food," Sagan said, coming into the kitchen. Cassidy jumped in surprise. "Sorry. I didn't mean to startle you. Hey, look at that feast. Aunt Patty outdid herself."

"Yes, it's a lovely dinner," Cassidy said, hoping her voice was steady. "How are you feeling, now that you've gotten up? I mean, now that you're moving around."

Sagan chuckled. "Pretty good. Sore in a million places, but everything seems to be in working order. Everything," he repeated, raising his eyebrows at her.

"Mmm," she said, then turned to pour steaming coffee into mugs. Battered and bruised, wearing faded cut-offs, an unbuttoned shirt, and tennis shoes with no socks, he was virile and rugged and gorgeous. Her heart was doing its usual flip-flops, and a hot desire was pulsing deep within her. She was a total wreck, darn him. "Sit down, Sagan."

He eased himself into the chair, then began to fill his plate. Cassidy brought the mugs to the table and sat opposite him.

"At least my war wounds are symmetrical," he said, buttering a biscuit. "The stitches are below the tape on the same side as the bummed-up rib. That means half of me is as good as new already. How're Chunky and the others?"

"Fine, I guess. Scrapes and bruises, and Joe Peter has two black eyes. They said they'd had worse. By the way, Harry finally showed up. He was the one who took us to the clinic in that godawful Jeep. He told the McKinneys he'd arrest them if he ever saw them in Cherokee again."

"Good for Harry," Sagan said, nodding. "Heard from Barry?"

"No. I don't know if that's good news or bad. I wish he'd call."

"That's got to be rough. You know, standing around waiting to find out if your wife and baby are going to be okay. Do they have family?"

"Back east. There's no one here or in Jasper."

"Damn. Well, maybe we could drive over there, give them a little moral support. What do you think?"

"That would be very nice, Sagan. It's a bumpy

road, though, as you well know. Wouldn't it be better to wait until you've had a few days to recuperate?"

"I suppose. Maybe Barry will report back in the meantime."

"Yes, I hope he does," she said. Oh, couldn't Sagan hear his own words? she thought with a flash of frustration. He was reaching out, caring about the people he'd met in Cherokee, just as they were reaching out to him. He knew how to love; he just didn't recognize it for what it was. Sagan could be sitting there at that very moment stuffing biscuits in his mouth and loving her for all he was worth. But if he didn't come out of the ether, chase away the fog, he might miss the whole thing.

They ate in silence for several minutes, making large dents in Aunt Patty's delicious food.

"You know," Sagan said finally, "I've been thinking about what you said before."

"What did I say?"

"That the only person around here who doesn't really know who I am, is me."

"And?"

"I don't buy it. I know who I am. I've kept myself on a very narrow path. My life has been simple and straightforward. Okay, so I'm a bit muddled since I met you, but that doesn't mean I don't know who I am. And while it's true that I'm not positive what I'm going to do with the rest of my life, I sure as hell know who I am."

"Well, for Pete's sake, don't get all in a snit about it."

"Well, hell, you made me sound like a borderline nut case."

"I did not. I was simply pointing out that—Oh, forget it. I'm not in the mood to argue with you, Sagan."

He leaned toward her. "What *are* you in the mood for?" he asked, his voice low.

"Fruit salad," she said, helping herself to another serving.

"Mmm." He glared at her.

"You're ruining your image, Jones. You're supposed to be the knight in shining armor. You've just slain the dragon to protect your lady's honor. Instead, you're a first-class grouch."

"I am? Oh. Well, I'm sorry. I'm new at this knight stuff. I'll get the hang of it, though. I'm a fast study."

"Hooray for you," Cassidy said dryly.

"Now who's a grouch?"

"Darn it, Sagan," she said, her voice rising, "if you're so quick, why can't you hurry up and learn how to be loved, then figure out what you're feeling for me, then—" She stopped speaking, plunked her elbow on the table, and rested her forehead in her hand. "Erase all that. That was so unfair, I can't believe it. I'm sorry, Sagan. I guess my nerves are shot. I'm going to clean up here, then take a long, relaxing bubble bath. I hope you didn't use all of my Nightly Sins." She got to her feet and carried her plate to the sink.

A moment later Sagan was behind her, wrapping his arm around her waist, and pulling her back against his uninjured side. She leaned her head on his shoulder and closed her eyes, savoring his heat, his strength, his aroma. Despite her nap, she was exhausted. She felt as though it were an effort to breathe.

"Ah, Cassidy," Sagan said, "what am I doing to you? Beaver asked me to stop by and check up on you, not disturb your serene existence or make you so damn sad. I don't have the right to do this to you. I refuse to feel guilty because we made love, but I never meant to take that sparkle from your eyes, the smile from your lips. I'll destroy your love for me and hurt you in the process."

"No. No, I—"

"I do that, you know," he said, his voice raspy. "Destroy people's love for me. I don't know why, I just do. My mother, then my father . . ." His voice trailed off.

Cassidy opened her eyes and turned in his embrace to face him. "Oh, Sagan, no," she said, her voice trembling. "I'm not like them. I'm not like your parents. Is that what you think? That something will happen, that you won't pass some test I've created in my mind, and I'll push a button and turn off my love for you? Oh, my God, what can I do to convince you that isn't true? I love you. I will always love you. Don't you believe me?"

He studied her face for a seemingly endless moment, searching for the answers to his questions. Cassidy watched his jaw tighten, saw anger flash through his dark eyes, then change to the bleakest despair and pain she'd ever seen. She choked back a sob as she mentally begged him to answer her, to say the words, tell her that he did believe in her and her love.

The seconds ticked by.

Then Sagan squared his shoulders and stepped back. He stepped back and created what was to

Cassidy a distance between them that she was incapable of crossing. He stepped back and didn't utter a single word. The silence screamed in the tiny room.

"Oh, Sagan," Cassidy whispered, hardly able to breathe, "I can't fight all the ghosts from the past. I'm not strong enough. I wouldn't know how. Oh, please, Sagan, don't do this to us. Don't make us pay the price for what they did to you so long ago."

He took another step backward, his eyes dark and haunted. His features were set in an unyielding mask, and Cassidy felt the distance between them grow wider and wider.

"I'm going for a walk," he said, turning toward the door. "Don't wait up." His voice was flat and hollow.

"You're supposed to be resting. Sagan, you're in no condition to—Sagan!" she shouted, running out of the kitchen.

But he was gone.

Cassidy pressed her fingertips to her lips to keep from calling his name again. Tears misted her eyes, and she barely avoided knocking over several plants as she stumbled to the sofa and sank onto it. Tears spilled freely onto her cheeks.

Strange, twisting pictures flitted through her mind as she sat alone in the quiet, darkening room. She saw Sagan as a little boy, reaching out his arms to a faceless man and woman. He was calling to them, but no sound came from his lips as they turned and walked away in opposite directions, disappearing into a hazy mist.

Then she saw Sagan grown; tall, strong, shoulders straight, the lift of his chin telling of his pride and determination. Through the mist a narrow path became clear, and he walked forward, no hesitation in his step. A circle of sunlight suddenly appeared, and within it stood Cassidy, smiling at him, opening her arms to embrace him.

The scenario in Cassidy's mind continued, the images so clear, it was as though it were all actually taking place. Sagan stopped on the path and looked at her, a gentle smile slowly softening his stern expression, his dark eyes glowing with desire and joy. She beckoned to him and he started toward her.

And then he stopped. He looked back in the direction from which he had come, then ahead into the mist, then redirected his attention to Cassidy. She smiled, nodded, urged him to come to her.

But he stepped back, shaking his head, his eyes dull and filled with pain. He looked at her for a long, heartrending moment, then continued his journey down the path, until the mist closed around him and he disappeared.

"No!" Cassidy said, getting to her feet. "It can't be like that." No! her mind thundered. Sagan had paid for his parents' cruelty all of his life. It was his turn to walk in the sunshine. It was his turn to trust and love and believe. And it was their turn. Sagan had shown her the full meaning of her womanhood, and with that knowledge had been born, she was sure, a wisdom only a woman could have. She would look deep within herself to find the key that would unlock the gate in the wall surrounding him. She possessed the weapon to beat the foes that held him in an iron grip. Its name was love.

Cassidy sank back onto the sofa, pulled her knees up, and wrapped her arms around them. She rested her chin on the steeple of her knees and stared unseeing across the room.

She would wait.

She would wait for Sagan to come home.

Sagan walked slowly, with no particular destination in mind. He simply planted one foot in front of the other and walked as the night closed in around him. His sore rib ached from the forced activity, but he didn't care. His stiff muscles loosened, became less painful, but he didn't care. The air was clear and cool, and the sky transformed itself into a canopy of twinkling stars, but he didn't care.

He was Sagan Jones. He was alone.

And he hated it.

What had suited him just fine for as long as he could remember, now crushed him with an oppressive weight.

Alone. Lonely. Empty. Cold. He walked on.

He avoided the main street of Cherokee, not wishing to see or speak to anyone. His long legs covered the ground quickly. He increased his pace, and Cherokee was soon at his back. His mind was a screaming jumble of voices, none clear, no message rising above the others, just a rushing noise not making any sense.

Time lost meaning, and still he walked. He questioned nothing when he changed directions, pushed his aching body to climb the hill before him, and the one after that. The moon was a silvery beacon lighting his way as he went on and on. He didn't know where he was going, knew only that he had to get there. He knew that sounded insane. But he didn't care.

And then he stopped. He drew a deep breath as he bent over, resting his hands on his thighs. The shuddering breath racked him with pain, his rib screamed for mercy, and he sank to his knees, then stretched out on his back with a groan.

He'd made it. He'd gotten there, to the place he had not even known he was struggling desperately to reach. He was lying in the wild flowers on the top of the hill where he'd first made love to Cassidy.

Sagan spread his arms wide on the ground, as if to gather in the memories of the ecstasy he'd shared there with her. It had been a joining of exquisite beauty, like nothing he had experienced before. Cassidy. It had been total giving and taking of pleasure too intense to describe in words. Cassidy. He had passed into her care the seed of his manhood and the soul of his inner being. Cassidy. They had been entwined in spirit as well as body—meshed, one, together.

Cassidy.

The stars twinkled a million hellos in the sky overhead, crickets serenaded in the distance, and the aroma of wild flowers filled his senses. Sagan welcomed Cassidy's image in his mind, embraced it, saw her smile, heard her laughter. His blood quickened at the thought of her.

He was alone on a hilltop, he mused, yet . . . he wasn't alone. Cassidy was there, warming him, telling him of her love for him, offering him all that she was and all that he'd never had. She was not of the past, but of now and of the future. He saw her in his mind's eye, reaching out to him, begging him to put to rest the ghosts that haunted him, to trust in her and her love, to rise above the pain of past promises broken . . . and believe.

She was Cassidy Cole. She was a golden cascade of silken hair, soft curves that fit perfectly against his hard body, a smile that lit up a room like sunshine itself. She was a funny clown in a green-and-yellow suit, and the epitome of femininity in the next instant. She rescued roosters with sore toes, and travel-weary strangers who appeared in her bathtub. She was unique, rare, special.

His. His Cassidy. And, dear God in heaven, he loved her.

The voices of confusion and fear within Sagan quieted, then stilled. Peace flowed throughout him like a comforting, soothing hand. The past disappeared into oblivion, never again to rear its ugly, destructive head.

The war within Sagan Jones was over.

Love had won.

Love for Cassidy Cole.

"My God," Sagan said, drawing a shaking hand down his sweat-soaked face. "I love her. I love Cassidy." His voice became louder, stronger. "I love Cassidy." He boomed his message to the night, and heard it echo back to him in all its splendor. "*I love Cassidy Cole!*"

Sagan's senses suddenly seemed sharper than ever before, bringing him the sights and sounds and smells of the enchanted night. He was acutely aware of every inch of his own body, knew its power and strength, his ability to protect Cassidy from harm.

He could feel the beating of his own heart, telling him that he was alive and healthy, and for the first time since he could remember, it mattered. He would care for and cherish and love his Cassidy for the remainder of his days. He wanted to leap to his feet and race down the hills to find her, tell her of his love and his desire to accept and treasure hers. He wanted to make love to her to seal a commitment of which he'd never dreamed he'd be a part.

But he'd have to wait, he knew, for he'd pushed his battered body to the limit to reach the hilltop of wild flowers, and first he'd have to rest.

Sagan laced his hands under his head and stared up at the star-studded sky. He knew he had a silly grin on his face, but he felt so damn good about life, about love, about Cassidy and Sagan as one. Love. He still didn't know exactly what his role was, how to be a half of a whole, a partner, he mused. But he'd figure it out. Nothing could stop him now. He was free of his past, and his future looked sensational.

"Oh, Cassidy," he said aloud, just to hear the sound of her name. He yawned. "Beautiful, beautiful Cassidy." His eyelids grew heavy. "I love you."

Then, right in the bed of flowers beneath the twinkling stars, Sagan slept.

Sunlight danced across Cassidy's face with insistent fingers, nudging her from the depths of sleep. She opened her eyes and blinked several times, feeling totally disoriented. Struggling to sit up, she realized that she was on her bed, still fully clothed.

Sagan, she thought, pushing aside the fogginess of sleep.

Her head snapped around to glimpse the empty pillow on the other side of the bed. No Sagan. During the night she must have stumbled into the bedroom and flung herself across the bed, but Sagan hadn't stumbled in after her. Unless . . .

Cassidy ran into the living room, skirting the plants, only to come to an abrupt halt as she saw the empty sofa. No Sagan.

Where was he? He was hurt, had no business being out of bed, let alone leaving the apartment. He'd said he was going for a walk. Where could he have been all night?

But even more important, was he coming back? Oh, dear heaven, had he left her forever?

"No, no, no," she said, shaking her head. "He wouldn't do that, would he?"

She went to the front door and opened it, looking out through the screen for any sign of him. Nothing. With a sigh that was closer to a sob, she walked numbly back into the bedroom, stripped off her clothes, then went into the shower. She shampooed her hair, then allowed the steaming water to beat against her body as her mind replayed, over and over, the scene with Sagan that had taken place just before he'd left.

He didn't believe in her love, she thought dismally. She was fighting such powerful ghosts from his past, and her firm resolve of the previous night to win his love was faltering fast. She didn't know what to do, she didn't know where he was, and she was miserable.

Cassidy stepped from the shower and sighed again. She sounded like a bike tire losing air, she thought.

The image fit. Without Sagan she would be empty, her life flat, just sitting there like a lump. Sagan filled her, made her complete, overflowing with happiness. And she could have done the same for him, given the chance. In her heart and soul she knew she could have brought him joy.

What if he had passed out, was lying in a ditch somewhere, had been overcome with pain and fatigue from his injuries? The thought of him out there alone, hurt, needing her, filled her with cold fear.

Cassidy wrapped one towel around her wet hair and another around her body. She'd go look for him, she decided. No, she'd wait here in case he came back. No, she'd . . . Oh, she didn't know what to do. Darn him, if he showed up she wouldn't know whether to hug him or hit him. *If* he showed up? Oh, he had to!

Cassidy opened the bathroom door, stepped into the bedroom, and froze.

Standing in the doorway to the bedroom, with a bouquet of wild flowers in his hand, was Sagan.

His hair was tousled, he needed a shave, and his shirt was still open and now badly wrinkled. His lip and eye were no longer swollen, but the flesh had turned twenty shades of purple. Cassidy thought he was the most beautiful sight she had ever seen.

"Sagan?" she whispered.

He walked slowly to the middle of the room, then stopped. "I . . . Um . . ." he said, "I brought you these flowers. They're from the hill where we . . . Our hill, where you were the princess, *my* princess."

"Thank you," she said. What a dumb thing to say,

she thought frantically. A casual "thank you" didn't quite suit the magnitude of the situation. But Sagan seemed tense, as though he were searching for the right words. She'd be patient, listen to what he had to say, and hope her heart hadn't shattered into a million pieces by the time he was finished.

"I'm very sorry if I worried you," he went on, "by staying away all night. I didn't mean to do that. I was sort of worn out by the time I got to our hill, and I fell asleep. I couldn't believe it when I woke up and—Am I babbling?"

"I think so."

"Oh," he said, raking a hand through his hair. "Okay, well, let me try again." He tossed the flowers onto a chair, then took a deep breath and let it out slowly. Cassidy's gaze was riveted on his face. "Cassidy, I realize I've turned your life upside down since I came here, but you did the same to mine."

"I'm sorry."

"No, no," he said quickly. "I'm not angry about it. Well, I was, but I'm not anymore. I was so damn confused. Questions were hammering at me, and I didn't know where to find the answers. My greatest fear was that my confusion would cause me to hurt you. Oh, Cassidy, I didn't want that to happen, but I wasn't sure I could stop it."

"I know, Sagan," she said softly.

"But then, last night, on our hilltop, beneath the stars, it all came together for me. It fell into place like a giant puzzle. I had a clear picture of everything for the first time." He stopped speaking, and swallowed hard. There was a line of sweat on his brow, and when he spoke again his voice was husky.

"Cassidy, I love you . . . so very much. I love you, and I believe in the love you're offering me, and I want to forget the past and look to the future with you, and—Dammit, say something!"

A gentle smile formed on Cassidy's lips, and tears misted her eyes as she walked slowly toward him. Stopping in front of him she could feel his heat, smell his aroma of fresh air, wild flowers, and grass, and the faint, heady scent of male perspiration. Her heart nearly burst with love as she saw the anxious expression on his face, the flicker of uncertainty in his dark eyes.

"Sagan," she said, her voice trembling, "those are the most beautiful words I have ever heard. I love you so much, Sagan. To have your love in return is the most precious gift I have ever received."

"Oh, thank God," he said with a groan, then reached out to pull her into his arms.

"Sagan, be careful. You're hurt, and—"

"Shh."

His mouth captured hers in a kiss so sweet, so tender, so sensuous, that Cassidy went nearly limp in his arms. He pulled the towel from her hair, and drew his fingers through the wet silken strands. The kiss intensified. The kiss spoke of commitment and forever, of a past forgotten and a future to be sought. The kiss sent desires soaring. The towel covering Cassidy's body fell to the floor.

Sagan's hands roamed over her moist, soft, fragrant skin as he fitted her to him, letting her feel the evidence of his arousal, his need and want, his love for her. His hands slid upward to cup her breasts, his thumbs teasing the nipples to taut buttons as he delved into her mouth with his tongue in a rhythmic motion.

Cassidy leaned into him, relishing the feel of his heated, heavy manhood pressing against her, savoring his taste, his strength, all that he was.

Sagan Jones loved her, her mind whispered, and the message was echoed by a joyous song from her heart. They had won, both of them. The prize was . . . forever.

"Let me love you," Sagan said, close to her lips. "I ache with wanting you. Oh, Cassidy, I do love you so much, so very much."

"And I love you. Come to me, Sagan."

Their joining was urgent, almost rough in its intensity. It was a need so great that it overpowered them both. Sagan shed his clothes, and then they tumbled onto the bed, reaching for each other, clinging to each other.

Cassidy vaguely remembered that Sagan was hurt, that they had to go slowly, gently, but the thought was fleeting as he moved over her, then into her with a thrust that took her breath away. And they flew—to their private place, their place of ecstasy. They flew, taking with them this time the knowledge of their shared love.

"Sagan!"

"Yes!"

They toppled over the edge into oblivion, calling to each other, declaring their love over and over. Their heartbeats slowly quieted, as did their labored breathing. Then Sagan pushed himself up on his forearms to look at Cassidy's flushed face.

"Incredible," he said. "It's always incredible with you."

"Oh, Sagan, I'm so happy. I was so frightened that I was going to lose you, and I love you so much. We have everything now. The future is at our fingertips. We . . . Sagan, are you all right? I don't think the doctor would have approved of what we just did."

He chuckled. "Actually," he said, moving off her, "I'm dying, but it was worth it. I couldn't have gone another minute without having you. Listen, we have to talk, make some plans, and—The phone is ringing."

"You stay put and rest. I'll get it."

Cassidy slipped off the bed, snatched a towel from the floor, and hurried into the living room as she wrapped the towel around her.

"Hello?" she said, after grabbing the receiver.

"Cassidy? Barry. Barbie's condition got worse, and the doctor decided he had to take the baby early, and he did, and everything is fine, and Barbie is just great, and the baby is little but perfect, and— Can you believe this? I have a son!"

"Barry, that's wonderful!"

"What's going on?" Sagan asked from the bedroom doorway.

"It's Barry. They had to take the baby early, but everything is fine. It's a boy. Barry," she said into the receiver, "what did you name him?"

"William Barry Howlett. Classy, huh? He weighs five pounds, three ounces. He sort of looks like a red prune, but I think he's terrific. Barbie came through it like a champ."

"Cassidy," Sagan said, "tell him we'll drive over today and see them."

"Are you sure, Sagan?"

"Yes. I need to do a couple of things in Jasper anyway."

"Barry, Sagan and I are driving over in a while to visit all of you."

"Great. See you when you get here. Call Aunt Patty for me, will you?"

"Of course. And I'll post a huge sign at Illusions tonight, announcing the arrival of William Barry Howlett. Oh, Barry, I'm thrilled for you. Kiss Barbie for me, and we'll see you soon. 'Bye."

Cassidy hung up the receiver and turned to face Sagan. "Oh, I'm so excited for them. What a wonderful day this is turning out to be. I'd better call Aunt Patty right away."

"Speaking of Aunt Patty, I guess it's time to tell you about my private business with her."

"Oh?"

"Do you remember that first night I stayed here, when you so kindly offered me your bed?"

"I was conned into sleeping on the sofa."

"Well, whatever. Anyway, I went for an early walk Saturday morning, remember?"

"Yes."

"Aunt Patty was out and about, and we were talking. Then along came the bus from Jasper, and on it were all my belongings. I couldn't believe they had caught up with me so fast. I knew I had no reason to stay here, because I'd said I was just waiting for my stuff. But I didn't want to leave. Something special was already happening between us, and I didn't want to go. I took my things to Aunt Patty's and hid them in her spare bedroom. So how much trouble am I in?"

Cassidy laughed. "You're a sneaky son of a gun, Sagan Jones. No wonder you bought Aunt Patty a cherry Coke with two cherries."

"And?"

"And," she said, smiling warmly, "I love you with every breath in my body."

"Come back into the bedroom."

"Don't you want some breakfast?"

"Later. Come into the bedroom."

"But you need to eat, regain your strength—"

"Cassidy!"

Her lilting laughter echoed through the room as she hurried to his side. Then, with his arm tightly circling her shoulders, they went into the bedroom.

Nine

The next few hours were a blur of activity. Aunt Patty was so excited about the new baby, Cassidy and Sagan immediately agreed that she should accompany them to Jasper for a peek at the Howlett heir.

During the drive, with Sagan behind the wheel of Cassidy's car, Cassidy asked Aunt Patty if the older woman was still using her spare bedroom for a sewing room. Sagan hooted with laughter, and told Aunt Patty he'd confessed his dastardly deed. Then, to Cassidy's wide-eyed amazement, he also told Aunt Patty that he and Cassidy were getting married.

"We are?" Cassidy asked. Her voice sounded like a squeaky hinge.

"Well, sure. I love you, you love me. We're getting married. Right?"

"Oh, this is wonderful," Aunt Patty gushed, clasping her hands together. "I knew everything was going to work out between you two. You're getting married. Oh, that's splendid."

"I know," Sagan said. "Right, Cassidy?"

"Oh, yes, right." She forced a smile. What was wrong with her? she wondered. Of course she wanted to marry Sagan. She loved him and he loved her, just as he'd said. Getting married was the natural thing to do. But, darn it, he could have asked her!

They hadn't talked about their plans for the future. She didn't know if Sagan even wanted to stay on in Cherokee, or what career he'd choose. Oh, she hated the idea of leaving her lovely little town, giving up Illusions, tromping off to heaven only knew where. They really needed to sit down and talk. About a lot of things. One of which was Sagan's officially asking her to become his wife. Oh, she was being silly, pouting again. They were going to be married, and that was what mattered. Still . . .

At the hospital in Jasper, the trio stopped first in the gift shop, where they purchased presents for the baby. Sagan picked out a football, and Cassidy rolled her eyes. Barry greeted them with a wide smile, and dragged them off to see his son through the nursery window.

"Oh, he's adorable," Cassidy said.

"Fine baby," Aunt Patty said, beaming. "Fine boy."

"Mmm," Sagan said, frowning and leaning closer to the glass.

"He'll smooth out," Barry assured them. "The wrinkles are temporary."

"I like his nose," Sagan remarked. "The kid has a state-of-the-art nose. When do you think he'll get some hair?"

"Beats me." Barry shrugged. "Look at the size of

those hands, Sagan. Is he a potential football player, or what?"

"Yep," Sagan agreed, "and I just got him his first football."

"Men are so weird," Cassidy whispered to Aunt Patty.

"By the way, Sagan," Barry asked, "what happened to your eye?"

"It's a long, grim story," Cassidy answered. "May we see Barbie now?"

Barry glanced at his watch. "In about ten minutes. She's in room four-ten. Sagan, what happened to your eye?"

"I'll tell you all about it over a beer," Sagan promised. "Come on, let's leave these ladies to their gossip."

"Okay," Barry said. "Cassidy, tell Barbie I'll be back soon."

"Shoo, then," Aunt Patty said. "We can't have any good girl talk with you two yahoos hanging around."

"We're gone." Sagan dropped a quick kiss on Cassidy's lips. " 'Bye. Hey, Barry, Cassidy and I are getting married."

"Really? That's great. Just think, next time we stand outside this window, we'll be looking at *your* baby."

"What!" Cassidy and Sagan chorused.

Barry laughed. "Buy me a beer, and I'll explain how it's done, Sagan. There's obviously something lacking in your education. Remember, Cassidy, tell Barbie I'll be back soon."

But Sagan and Barry weren't back soon.

Cassidy and Aunt Patty had a lovely visit with Barbie before being asked to leave because it was William Barry Howlett's feeding time. Cassidy bought

Aunt Patty a cup of coffee in the cafeteria, and then they returned to the maternity floor, where they were told Barbie was sleeping.

Cassidy glanced often at her watch, hoping that Sagan was remembering to do the same. They had a long drive ahead of them, and she wanted to open Illusions on time.

"They'll be along," Aunt Patty said as Cassidy paced the waiting-room floor. "They're probably really celebrating Barry's first son."

Cassidy halted. "They're getting drunk?"

"Wouldn't surprise me any."

"Wonderful." Cassidy threw up her hands. "That's all I need. Sagan claims that he feels well enough to tend bar tonight, but he won't be able to if he's blitzed."

When they arrived an hour later, Sagan and Barry weren't drunk.

"Let's go," Sagan said abruptly. "We've got to get to Cherokee so we can open Illusions on time. See ya, Barry."

"Keep me posted, Sagan. Thanks for coming, Cassidy, Aunt Patty. I'll let you know when we're coming home."

"Cassidy, come on," Sagan said, striding off down the hall on his long legs. "We're running late."

"I'm going to give him a matching set of black eyes," she muttered. "I swear I am." Aunt Patty laughed in delight.

During the drive back to Cherokee, Cassidy refused to ask Sagan where he had been with Barry, and he offered no explanation. The conversation was made up primarily of Aunt Patty's chatter. After dropping Aunt Patty at home, Sagan drove above the speed limit to Cassidy's apartment.

As she headed for the kitchen, she said, "We don't have time for much of a dinner. Is another omelet okay?"

"Sure," Sagan agreed. "I'll set the table." He followed her into the kitchen.

"I wish we had time to talk." Cassidy opened a cupboard and peered in. "Where's my frying pan?"

"I wish we had time for other things," Sagan said, flashing her a dazzling smile.

"I'm serious, Sagan," she said, opening another cupboard. "Where's the frying pan? There are things we need to discuss. Where in hell's bells is my frying pan?"

"Frying pan? Uh-oh."

"Uh-oh?" She turned to look at him. "Why would you say 'uh-oh' about my frying pan?"

"Because it's in the oven."

"Oh," she said, reaching for the handle on the oven door.

"But I didn't wash it," he rushed on.

She flung open the oven door, and snatched up the frying pan. "Oh, yuck. It has a dread disease. How could you do this?"

Sagan laughed. "I'll scrub it right now, okay?"

"I refuse to use that disease-laden pan," she said, lifting her chin.

"Oh, for crying out loud." Sagan turned on the hot water. "I'll spit-shine this baby."

"Speaking of babies," Cassidy said stiffly, "are you ready to explain where you were all afternoon while Aunt Patty and I were visiting Barbie?"

"Oh, that." Sagan shrugged. He began to scour

the pan. "I bought Barry a beer to celebrate his son's arrival. Then we got to talking about the idea of serving sandwiches and dessert at Illusions."

"I thought you were going to work up a cost-analysis report first and let me see it."

"I'm still going to do the report. It's the only smart way to operate. Thing is, Barry knew where to find the kind of people I needed. I have to compare the cost of making the stuff right at Illusions, and having it brought over from Jasper." He patted his back pocket. "I have all the figures right here. Now all I have to do is project them and write up my findings."

"I see," Cassidy said quietly.

"Barry was big on the idea. He'd like nothing better than to go into Illusions on an earlier shift so he'd be home for more of the evening with Barbie and . . . Do you suppose they're going to call that kid Billy? Barbie, Barry, and Billy. That's a bit much. Oh, well. Anyway, Barry agrees that there are real possibilities for expansion at Illusions. He's eager to see the figures I come up with. I should have the report ready by the time he gets back to Cherokee. Don't forget to give me the account books. There, Cassidy, take a gander at this frying pan. There isn't a germ brave enough to be in the same room with it."

"Sagan, I'd like to see the cost report, too, you know," she said, a slight edge to her voice.

"Sure. Listen, I'll go take a quick shower while you toss some eggs in this spiffy pan." He gave her a peck on the lips. "I'll be right back."

Cassidy glanced at the doorway, at the frying pan, and then at the doorway again. She must look like a cartoon heroine about to whop the cartoon hero over the head with a frying pan, she thought. The idea had definite appeal.

Cassidy was frowning as she started to prepare the omelet. She wished Sagan would slow down a bit. He was moving full steam ahead, and she felt as though she were running in place, unable to keep up with him.

She was full of contradictions, she admitted. When she had been so filled with the fear that Sagan would leave her, she'd wanted him to hurry up and solve his inner turmoil. She'd wanted him to snap his fingers and declare himself to be all squared away, in one quick moment. It had seemed like an eternity before Sagan had come to her and said he loved her. Time had dragged by with agonizing slowness as she'd waited, filled with longing and uncertainty.

But now? Now he *had* declared his love for her, along with his willingness to accept her love in return. The memory of him standing in her bedroom holding the wild flowers from their hilltop and telling her about his feelings was tucked away in a special chamber of her heart.

But, darn it, Sagan had to slow down and talk to her. She felt as though she were on the outside of her own life looking in, and everyone knew what was going on but her.

"Is dinner ready?" Sagan asked, coming back into the kitchen.

"Yes."

"Good. Eat fast."

"Sagan, there are things we need to discuss." She sat down opposite him at the table.

"We will, but not now. There's no time. So break it

to me gently. What's the illusion at Illusions on Monday night?"

"A zoo."

"What?"

"Animals. A zoo. We all dress up as different animals. Get it?"

He squinted at her. "What kind of costumes? How skimpy is yours?"

Cassidy shrugged. "That's a hard question to answer. You know, skimpy is in the eye of the beholder."

"Eat faster, then go put it on. I want to see this creation. What kind of animal are you?"

"A bunny," she said, then shoveled in a forkful of omelet.

"Bunny," Sagan repeated slowly. "Not good. A lot of oil drillers get magazines sent to them overseas, Cassidy. I've seen pictures of some unbelievable bunnies."

"Shame on you."

"Do you have a tail?"

"I beg your pardon?"

"A tail," he repeated, leaning toward her. "A fuzzy tail right on your tush that wiggles when you walk."

"Well, yes, I have a tail. How can I be a bunny without a tail?"

"I don't like this," he said, glaring at her.

"You haven't even seen it yet. You're doing your macho routine again, Sagan."

"Damn right I am." He smacked the table with his hand. Cassidy jumped. "You're my lady. You're going to be my wife. I don't want a bunch of guys looking at your tail."

"Oh, for Pete's sake," she said, getting to her feet. "I'll go change right now."

"I'll clean the kitchen."

"And don't you dare put the frying pan in the oven," she said as she started toward the door. Sagan chuckled.

In the bedroom, Cassidy took the pink bunny suit from the closet and laughed softly as she held it at arm's length in front of her. She knew she could have eased Sagan's mind at the start of the conversation, but the temptation to tease had been too great.

There was nothing sexy or suggestive about a fuzzy pink bunny suit fashioned like a baby's sleeper, complete with feet.

Cassidy zipped herself into her outfit, coiled a single braid around the top of her head, and went into the living room.

"Saa-gan," she called in a syrupy-sweet voice. "Your little ole bunny is ready for your little ole inspection, darlin'."

Sagan wasted no time coming from the kitchen. He stopped so quickly, he nearly fell over his own feet. He laughed. He laughed so hard that he had to lean against the wall for support. He laughed until he was groaning and clutching his injured rib. The boisterous sound was infectious, and Cassidy's smile widened. She, too, laughed until she had to gasp for breath.

And then, somehow, she was in Sagan's arms, and in the next instant he was kissing her, his hands roaming over the soft material covering her body. The kiss was long and powerful, and Cassidy's heart was racing when he finally released her.

"Interesting zipper," he said huskily as his gaze

traveled down the suit. "I'll check that out more thoroughly when we get home."

"After we talk," she said firmly.

"Mmm," he said, his heated gaze making its way back upward until their eyes met. "That is some illusion, kid. You look about eight years old, but I know—oh, lady, do I ever know—how much of a woman you are beneath that crazy thing. *My* woman. And I love you, Cassidy."

"Oh, Sagan," she whispered.

"The door," he said, pointing to it.

Cassidy batted her eyelashes at him, then headed for the door with an exaggerated sway of her hips that caused her fuzzy tail to wiggle vigorously. Sagan swatted at it playfully as they left the apartment.

Cassidy's lighthearted mood began to fade almost immediately after she arrived at Illusions. In addition to the sign she hung, announcing the birth of William Barry Howlett, Sagan hung one of his own, stating that Cassidy Cole was to marry Sagan Jones. Soon Illusions was one huge party celebrating the double dose of good news. Cassidy smiled until her cheeks ached. But she was acutely aware of her uneasiness and the knot in her stomach.

Nothing was wrong, she told herself. Yet everything was wrong. She felt as though she were losing control of her life and . . . She had to stop this! Sagan loved her. They were going to be married.

"Hey, Sagan," Chunky said at around midnight. "What's the plan? You're staying on in Cherokee, aren't you? You and Cassidy aren't cutting out for the big city, are you?"

Cassidy stiffened. She turned to look at Sagan, who placed a bottle of beer in front of Chunky with a wide smile.

"Damn right we're staying on in Cherokee," Sagan said, circling Cassidy's shoulders with his arm. "Big-city life has nothing to offer us. Besides, Chunky, where else can I be in a beauty of a brawl and not end up in jail?"

The two men laughed. Then Sagan moved away from Cassidy to fix the drinks that Carmen, in a tiger costume, was waiting for.

A chill swept through Cassidy, and a strange rushing noise roared in her ears. They were staying in Cherokee? This was the first she knew about it, yet Sagan hadn't hesitated a moment in answering Chunky's question. Sagan obviously had their future all mapped out, to the smallest detail. What was she supposed to do, trail behind him like his shadow, and pick up clues as they went along? Damn the man. She'd had enough of this!

The next hour dragged by, and Cassidy found herself clenching her jaw so hard, her teeth ached. As the minutes ticked away, her anger grew, and her smile was stiff and forced when she waved good-bye to everyone at closing time.

"Whew," Sagan said in the sudden silence. "This was quite a night."

"Yes, it certainly was," Cassidy said coolly, not looking at him.

"I'll wash these glasses while you wipe off the tables. Then we'll go home. Are you all right? You're awfully pale."

"We'll talk at home, Sagan," she said, moving out from behind the bar.

"Sure." He frowned. He watched her attack the tables with a vengeance.

During the ride to the apartment, Cassidy clasped her hands tightly together in her lap and stared out the side window. She could feel Sagan's eyes on her. He glanced over at her often, but neither spoke. At the apartment, she went directly into the bedroom, changed out of her bunny suit into a robe, and brushed her hair free. Taking a deep breath, she went back into the living room. Sagan still stood in front of the closed door, his hands now shoved into his back pockets.

"Okay," he said, "spill it. What's wrong? You're so tense, I can practically hear you crackling."

She stopped across the room from him. "Sagan, please try to understand. We're not talking, sharing, communicating. I keep finding out about our plans by hearing you tell someone else. I feel like an outsider, and I'm supposed to be half of all this. You told Aunt Patty we were getting married, but you never asked me. You moved ahead with the plans for Illusions with Barry instead of with me. You told Chunky that we were staying in Cherokee. I didn't know that. How could I? We never discussed it."

Sagan frowned deeply, then shook his head as though he didn't quite believe what he'd just heard.

"You're ticked off because we're getting married, might expand Illusions, and are staying in Cherokee?"

"No!"

He pulled his hands free and folded his arms over his chest. "Do you intend to marry me?" he asked, a tight muscle twitching in his jaw.

"Yes, of course, but—"

"Do you want to live here in Cherokee?"

"Yes, but—"

"If my findings prove that expanding Illusions would mean greater profits, would that bother you?"

"No, but—"

"Then what in the hell is your problem?" he roared. "Dammit, I told you I didn't know how to be in love, be half of a whole, but how can making you happy be wrong? Tell me, Cassidy. Just how in the hell can that be wrong?"

"You don't understand."

"You've got that part right, lady," he said, raking a hand through his hair. "All these decisions meet with your almighty approval, but you're still passing judgment on me. I knew all this was right for you, for us, but what am I supposed to do? Stand around while you decide if I've screwed it up?"

"I want to be included in the decision making, Sagan," she said firmly.

"Ah, hell," he said, staring up at the ceiling. "This is ridiculous."

"Sagan," she said, her voice suddenly hushed, "please listen to me. I love you. I love you so much. But do you know how I felt when I heard you telling someone else about our future?" She drew a shaky breath. "I was lonely."

Sagan stared down at her. "What?"

"Alone and lonely," she said, her voice beginning to tremble. "I love you, but I also need you. I need to share, to be a part of all that we are. I felt as though I were being pushed to the outside to look in. It's cold out here, Sagan. And so very, very lonely."

"Oh, dear Lord," he said, pain evident on his face, in his dark eyes. "I never meant . . . I thought I was doing the right things for you. I don't know how to do this at all, don't you see? Lonely? With me? Because of me? I've hurt you already, and we've hardly begun. I'll go on hurting you, too, because I don't know how not to."

Cassidy hardly breathed as she listened to him, heard the anguish in his voice, saw the pain etched on his rugged features. What had she done? She *had* stood in judgment on him. She *had* treated him as though he'd failed a test. She had decided how things should be done by two people in love, then raged in anger when Sagan hadn't followed the program.

She'd expected him to know he should discuss things with her, just as he'd expected her to know his decisions had been made with her happiness in mind.

"Oh, Sagan," she whispered, "I'm so sorry."

"What?" he said, looking confused. "*You're* sorry? I'm the one who blew it."

"No. No, you didn't. I was just as guilty of . . . No, wait. We're not guilty or wrong. Oh, Sagan, we're *learning* how to love, be in love, to share, be one. We have to learn how to speak aloud what's in our hearts and minds, talk to each other. I realize now that I don't know how to be in love, either, Sagan, but we can learn together, if we try, and have patience with each other. We've got so much—our love, our future, everything. We'll be together always, and we'll never, ever be lonely."

"Oh, Cassidy," he said, holding out his arms to her, "come here."

She ran across the room and was caught by his strong arms, remembering at the last minute not to fling herself against his injured side. He buried his face in the fragrant cloud of her hair as she circled his neck with her arms. They held each other, simply held each other, drawing strength and happiness from each other.

Sagan slowly lifted his head to look down at her, making no attempt to hide the tears glistening in his eyes.

"I love you," he said, his voice taut with emotion. "You are my life. I thought . . . I thought everyone knew how to love except me."

"We'll learn together, Sagan," she said, tears spilling onto her cheeks. "Our love isn't an illusion. It's real. It will grow stronger with every passing day."

"And every passing night?" he asked, managing a smile.

"Come with me, Mr. Jones." She took his hand, smiling through her tears. "There's one area of our lives that needs no discussion at all."

Epilogue

Cassidy reached the top of the hill and filled her lungs with the scent of wild flowers. She shielded her eyes with her hand and surveyed the framework of the large house under construction.

"Sagan?" she called.

"Yes!"

"I brought a picnic lunch for us."

"On my way."

She watched him approach, drinking in the sight of his bare chest, his jeans slung low on his narrow hips, and felt the curl of hot desire deep within her.

Beautiful, beautiful Sagan.

Sagan stopped in front of her, slid his hand to the nape of her neck, and pulled her forward to receive a long, powerful kiss that caused her knees to tremble.

"Hello, Mrs. Jones," he said, his breathing rough.

"Hello, Mr. Jones," she answered breathlessly. "How's the work going?"

"Great. I never thought I'd use those house plans,

but there's the house, going up little by little. And on our hilltop, too. You, princess, will be able to sit up here and watch over your subjects." He tugged on her hand, and they sank to the carpet of flowers. "What's for lunch?"

Cassidy opened the wicker basket she had brought along. "Where's Beaver?"

"He went to Jasper for copper wire. Carmen's going with him, so I doubt that he'll be back today." He peered into the basket. "Champagne?"

"Yep. This is our anniversary."

"It is not. I know when we were married, Cassidy. This is not our anniversary."

"Yes, it is. One year ago today we made love for the first time in these flowers on this hill."

"Oh, *that* anniversary," he said, chuckling. "I'll drink to that."

"It's been a glorious year, Sagan," she said, placing her hand on his cheek. "We've done it, you know. We've learned how to love."

"I'd say we're getting the hang of it." He turned his head to place a kiss on her palm. "Yep, it's been a great year. Illusions is serving full lunches and dinners, our house is well underway, and your nutty brother never got around to leaving after our wedding."

Cassidy laughed. "Beaver is so in love with Carmen, he can't see straight. I wish he'd quit messing around and ask her to marry him."

"Ask her," Sagan said, nodding. "That's how it's supposed to be done. I never did ask you to marry me. Cassidy, will you marry me?"

"I did."

"I know, but I'm taking care of all my past mistakes."

"We discuss everything now, Sagan," she said, sliding her hands up his chest. She leaned forward and outlined his lips with her tongue. "Every little detail."

"Is this a discussion?" he asked, his breathing becoming labored.

She popped open the snap on his jeans. "It certainly is." Her fingers inched inside the soft denim.

"What's the—Cassidy!—subject?"

"A baby."

"A who?" he asked with a croak. "Get your hand out of there. A baby? You want a baby?"

"Don't you?"

"Yes, I do. I really do. If you don't quit wiggling your fingers like that . . . Is this discussion over yet? Did we just agree to have a baby?"

"Yes, Mr. Jones, I believe we did."

"Then, Mrs. Jones," he said, lowering her back onto the bed of flowers, "the discussion part of this meeting is over. It's time to get down to serious business. Here, on this hilltop, in these flowers. Perfect."

"Perfect," Cassidy echoed in a whisper, then opened her arms to receive Sagan into her embrace.

THE EDITOR'S CORNER

February is a favorite LOVESWEPT month. After all, it's the month dedicated to love and romance—and that's what we're all about! Romance is (and should be!) more important in our lives than just one special day, so LOVESWEPT is claiming February as a whole month dedicated to love. What a wonderful world it would be if we could convince everyone!

In this special month, we have six marvelous books with very pretty covers. In our LOVESWEPT Valentine month we have given all of our books covers in pink/red/purple shades—from pale pink confection, to hot fuschia pink, to red-hot-red, and passionate purple. This is our way of celebrating the month—so be sure to look for the SHADES OF LOVESWEPT covers, and we know you'll enjoy all the stories inside.

Our first book for the month, **STIFF COMPETITION**, LOVESWEPT #234, by Doris Parmett, is a heart-warming and very funny story about next door neighbors who are determined not to fall in love! Both Stacy and Kipp have been burned before and they go to ridiculous lengths to maintain their single status! But he can't resist the adorable vixen next door and she can't stop thinking of the devil-may-care hero of her dreams. When Kipp finally takes her in his arms, their resistance is swept away by sizzling passion and feel-

(continued)

The first Delaney trilogy

Heirs to a great dynasty, the Delaney brothers were united by blood, united by devotion to their rugged land . . . and known far and wide as

THE SHAMROCK TRINITY

Bantam's bestselling LOVESWEPT romance line built its reputation on quality and innovation. Now, a remarkable and unique event in romance publishing comes from the same source: THE SHAMROCK TRINITY, three daringly original novels written by three of the most successful women's romance writers today. Kay Hooper, Iris Johansen, and Fayrene Preston have created a trio of books that are dynamite love stories bursting with strong, fascinating male and female characters, deeply sensual love scenes, the humor for which LOVESWEPT is famous, and a deliciously fresh approach to romance writing.

THE SHAMROCK TRINITY—Burke, York, and Rafe: Powerful men . . . rakes and charmers . . . they needed only love to make their lives complete.

☐ *RAFE, THE MAVERICK by Kay Hooper*

Rafe Delaney was a heartbreaker whose ebony eyes held laughing devils and whose lilting voice could charm any lady—or any horse—until a stallion named Diablo left him in the dust. It took Maggie O'Riley to work her magic on the impossible horse . . . and on his bold owner. Maggie's grace and strength made Rafe yearn to share the raw beauty of his land with her, to teach her the exquisite pleasure of yielding to the heat inside her. Maggie was stirred by Rafe's passion, but would his reputation and her ambition keep their kindred spirits apart?   (21846 • $2.75)

LOVESWEPT

☐ *YORK, THE RENEGADE by Iris Johansen*

Some men were made to fight dragons, Sierra Smith thought when she first met York Delaney. The rebel brother had roamed the world for years before calling the rough mining town of Hell's Bluff home. Now, the spirited young woman who'd penetrated this renegade's paradise had awakened a savage and tender possessiveness in York: something he never expected to find in himself. Sierra had known loneliness and isolation too—enough to realize that York's restlessness had only to do with finding a place to belong. Could she convince him that love was such a place, that the refuge he'd always sought was in her arms?

(21847 • $2.75)

☐ *BURKE, THE KINGPIN by Fayrene Preston*

Cara Winston appeared as a fantasy, racing on horseback to catch the day's last light—her silver hair glistening, her dress the color of the Arizona sunset . . . and Burke Delaney wanted her. She was on his horse, on his land: she would have to belong to him too. But Cara was quicksilver, impossible to hold, a wild creature whose scent was midnight flowers and sweet grass. Burke had always taken what he wanted, by willing it or fighting for it; Cara cherished her freedom and refused to believe his love would last. Could he make her see he'd captured her to have and hold forever?

(21848 • $2.75)